To-Ho
and the Gold Destroyers

Also by Jules Lermina:

Panic in Paris
(*translated by Brian Stableford*)

To-Ho
and the Gold Destroyers

by
Jules Lermina

adapted in English by
George T. Dodds

A Black Coat Press Book

Acknowledgements: Thanks to Marc Madouraud.

Visit our website at www.blackcoatpress.com

Introduction

To-Ho, le Tueur d'Or [translated here as *To-Ho and the Gold Destroyers*] was first published in 1905 in *Le Journal des Voyages*, 2nd Series, Nos. 448-470. The monumental weekly had started publication in 1875 as *Sur Terre et Mer* [*On Land & On Sea*], then took its definitive title in 1877. Its publishing history spanned over 70 years:

- 1st series (1877-1896), 1012 issues published;
- 2nd series (1896-1915): 941 issues published;
- 3rd series (1924-25): 29 issues published;
- 4th series (1925-29): 159 issues published; and
- 5th series (1946-1949): 149 issues published.

As its title indicated, it was the natural home for Vernian tales dealing with exotic lands and uncanny adventures in which daring heroes and their virginal girlfriends fought would-be masters of the world and mad scientists, often of Germanic or Asian origins. That chauvinistic, somewhat xenophobic, yet visionary magazine serialized novels by Louis Boussenard, Paul d'Ivoi, René Thévenin, Albert Bonneau (often writing as "Maurice Champagne"), G. Le Wailly, Capitaine Danrit and Jules Lermina.

Jules Hippolyte Lermina was born in 1839 and was still a child when the revolution of 1848 was followed by Louis Napoléon's *coup d'état*, which launched in the Second Empire in 1851. He grew up to be a dedicated opponent of that Empire, working from a radical socialist viewpoint. Having married at 18, with a baby daughter to support, he tried his hand at various clerical jobs, but either could not settle into them or—perhaps more likely—could not hold on to them because of his political opinions and turned his hand to freelance journalism instead. His radicalism was just as hazardous in that vocation as any other employment, by virtue of the relentless vigilance and oppressive policies of Napoléon III's censors, and he soon attracted their attention. He founded a political periodical of his own, *Le Corsaire*, in 1867, which led to his being imprisoned. He was soon released in response to protest—from Victor Hugo, among others—but promptly repeated his crime, founding a new journal called *Satan*, and was imprisoned again.

By this time, the Second Empire was on its last legs, and it finally collapsed in 1870 following the disastrous French defeat by the Prussian army in the Battle of Sedan. Lermina was released from prison as soon as the new Government of National Defense took office, and promptly enlisted, either by virtue of a surge of patriotic fervor or because it was a condition of his release. He was only in uniform for a matter of months, but must have had a terrible time. He was far from being a natural soldier—he was short, thin, pale, puny and of a somewhat nervous disposition even when not fresh out of prison—and his regiment, which engaged the enemy on at least two occasions, had no chance whatsoever of stemming the Prussian tide.

Military discipline did not shut Lermina up. He prepared campaign literature with which to stand for elections to the new National Assembly, before the promised elections were cancelled, and wrote an angry open letter of protest to the government when the chief protagonists of Communist agitation were imprisoned. Had he not been busy fighting the Prussians, however, he would almost certainly have taken a hand in the sub-

sequent insurrection, and might well have been transported along with its leaders when the Commune fell. As
things were, the whole experience seems to have been
rather traumatic, and he took a new direction in life thereafter. One source suggests that he became involved in
a project to form the communist colony of Aiglemont in
the Ardennes, but if so his participation was brief; he
was soon back in Paris, where—perhaps taking some
inspiration from the oft-imprisoned activist and prolific
feuilletoniste Louis Ulbach—he launched a new phase of
his career, concentrating on popular fiction.

Although Lermina's left-wing views did not
change, he seems to have contented himself for the next
decade with simply making a living, and his subsequent
political journalism was more reflective in kind. He was
still writing regularly for *Le Radical* in the 1890s,
though, and his most significant work in that vein, the
anarchist *L'ABC du Libertaire* [*The ABC of Libertarian-
ism*] did not appear until 1906. His political beliefs are
manifest in some of his fiction, including in *To-Ho*, in
which a noble savage, who is one of Tarzan's more significant literary precursors, declares war on the symbolic
foundation of capitalism, but the great bulk of his fiction
consisted of crowd-pleasing entertainment in the great
tradition of the French *roman feuilleton*. He consciously
set out to be a loyal disciple of Eugène Sue and Alexandre Dumas; he wrote a Suesque *Mystères de New York*
under the pseudonym William Cobb and produced two
sequels to *Le Comte de Monte Cristo*, as well as many
other works in the same vein, almost all of which are
nowadays long-forgotten.

Jules Clarétie, who wrote an introduction to Lermina's first collection of fantastic tales, *Histoires incroyables* [*Incredible Stories*] (1885), records that he

7

and his friend had both been strongly influenced in their early days by E. T. A. Hoffmann and Edgar Allan Poe, the presiding geniuses of the 19th century French *fantastique*, and that they had both attempted work of that sort when they launched their careers in 1859. Almost all the work that Lermina published in the first phase of his journalistic career and his first decade as a *feuilletoniste* was, however, naturalistic, in accordance with the prevailing priorities of the marketplaces in which he worked. The first scientific romance that Versins credits to him is a horror story based on a popular urban myth about the persistence of consciousness in decapitated heads, "*La peine de mort*" [*The Death Penalty*] (1868), but the next is dated 1884—although Versins appears to have overlooked "*L'Arbre anthropophage*" [*The Man-Eating Tree*] (1878; reprinted in *Nouvelles histoires incroyables*, 1888, as "*Titane*"). Lermina also published a Poesque tale of psychological disturbance before his second term of imprisonment, "*Les fous*" [*The Madmen*] (*Le Gaulois*, 1869; reprinted in *Histoires incroyables*), which was set in America and signed "William Cobb," and some of the other stories in the two collections of *histoires incroyables* might have seen first publication at similarly early dates. "*Les fous*" had the distinction of attracting praise from Isidore Ducasse, *alias* Lautréamont, who mentioned it in his *Poésies* (1870)

Although the items in *Histoires incroyables* and *Nouvelles histoires incroyables* are mostly offbeat horror stories, some are frankly parodic and most of them are liberally spiced with ironic wit. Although this aspect of his work was clearly influenced by Poe, as emphasized by the frequent use of American settings and an Anglo-Saxon pseudonym, Lermina's fantasies tended to exploit the humorous aspects of the grotesque and arabesque to a greater extent than the earnestly horrific, and he seems to have been strongly infected by what Poe called "the imp of the perverse." His interested in the *incroyable* did, however, increase markedly in the mid-1880s, when he became temporarily involved with the burgeoning occult revival. Jules Clarétie, who shared that involvement, became earnestly fascinated with spiritualism, eventually becoming a regular at Camille Flammarion's *salons* and *séances*, but Lermina's initial involvement seems to have been entirely accidental.

Although he had sold stories to the first series of the *Journal des Voyages*, Lermina became a much more frequent presence in its second series. Most of his contributions were straightforward adventures stories of a melodramatic stripe, similar to those he had earlier contributed to the less adventurous *Terre Illustrée*, but he also provided such lively and interesting serial scientific romances as *To-Ho* and *Mystère-Ville* [*Mysteryville*] (1904 as by William Cobb; to be translated in a future Black Coat Press volume).

It was during this final phase of his career that Lermina produced *L'Effrayante aventure* (1910; translated as *Panic in Paris*, Black Coat Press, 2009), which appeared amid a glut of French scientific romances inspired by the example of the British writer H. G. Wells; Lermina would probably have done more in the same vein had he been able to do so, but was then reaching the end of his career and his life; he died in 1915.

Brian Stableford

Part One: Mayha's Torments

Chapter I

In the *kraton* [1] of Kota-Rajia, rising ærie-like above the Kroung-Daroub river, on the northern headland of the island of Sumatra, the Orang Aceh defended themselves against the Dutch conquerors with a courage born of desperation.

People of violent manners, with an instinct for pillage, the Aceh seemed untamable; their Sultan, Mahmoud Shah, shut up in the lofty and savage *kraton* fortress, perched upon a mass of inaccessible crag, fended off all attacks, directing with a savage energy his troops, whose corpses afforded an impenetrable barrier. About the Master, Servant of Allah, the chiefs of barbaric and fearless tribes were assembled. Fanatical, contemptuous of death, they forgot their internecine quarrels in this ultimate crisis, gathering hastily to offer resistance to the invader.

All were in attendance: the cattle-slaughterers of Wasla; the *oobo-oobo*, jellyfish and octopus-eaters of Malaboch; the Malivang, come forth from the impenetrable gorges of Lake Tola; even those of Tibab on the southern headland, near the Straits of Sund. Hatred of the foreigner, of the civilized, the *roumi*, [2] united these most disparate of peoples under the acknowledged au-

---

[1] An Indonesian name for palace.
[2] Christian or foreigner.

11

thority of the Sultan's three great *panglimas* [3]: Toukou Ibrahim, Lord of the 26 *moukims*; [4] Toukou Polim, who commanded 22 *moukims*; and Toukou Lampasay, chief of 25.

For nine years, the war had raged, tenacious and indefatigable on the part of the Dutch, furious and desperate by the Aceh, audacious pirates who repelled the intrusion of Europeans, the detested white man. For centuries, sheltered in the deep coves of their rivers, they had watched the ships. Like albatross, they would suddenly and without warning swoop down on them. Their pillaging and murderous ways terrorized the Indian Ocean and Straits of Malacca. The islands of Bali, Nias and Raopat were nothing but a nest of pirates, from which, every day, these vultures of the sea came forth, making passage impossible. Oulaylay, the port of Kota-Rajia, was the lair from which the Aceh pirates sprang. Edi, on the strait, threatened the merchant marine headed for Singapore.

After long parleys, after small battles in which the advantage had remained with the Aceh, the Dutch has decided to expend an ultimate effort. In 1872, a first ultimatum had been sent to the sultan, who had answered with insolent bravado; by 1878, the attack had begun in earnest, and powerful artillery was bombarding Oulaylay. Yet, before the powerful Aceh resistance, the Dutch had had to fall back.

General Kohler, leader of the expedition, had been killed; then, after him, Colonel van Gogh, then General van Swieten, who, for an instant, had believed these untamable people tamed, until he encountered a new, even

---

[3] Tribal leaders or lieutenants.
[4] Districts.

more determined, revolt, had perished too. During a raid into the 26 *moukims*, General Pel fell, according to some in an apoplectic fit, but according to more sinister but plausible rumors, poisoned. Finally, General Dianout, giving up on victory, gave up the fight, leaving Colonel van der Hyeden in command.

And now, the supreme test had come: at Samalaga, the Colonel, shot in the head, blinded by blood, had stayed on the battlefield until the trumpets had told him of the victory. For the first time, before this man who seemed to cheat death, a breath of fear had wafted over the lands of the Aceh. One sensed that the hour of truth was at hand.

That day, on the great square before the *kraton*, where the invisible and still-feared Sultan stood, the leaders had gathered the men and their tribes. The news of a new defeat had arrived: 100 Battaks had been surrounded in the bed of a ravine and had been massacred to the last. This was a fierce and pitiless war. The Acehs' fury turned to madness: men, frenzied, *kriss* [5] in hand, drove through the crowd as if drunk or epileptic, wounding and killing all those they could lay their hands on. It was the *amok*, the Malaysians' bloody delirium which burst out under this paroxysm of despair.

The *panglima* of Pedir, a superbly proportioned, giant of a warrior, had leapt to the stele, the remains of some ancient Buddhist pagoda, and, his two fists raised to the sky, brandishing a serrated saber, cried vengeance:

"No! We, the free Orangs, shall never retreat before the eternal enemy! There must be erected, in every corner of the land, *beatangs* [6] from whence poisoned arrows

---

[5] Indonesian asymmetrical dagger.
[6] Improvised redoubts.

can fly. Each tree, each fold in the terrain, will conceal an avenger! No one is to lose courage, ever! For every child of Aceh fallen, thousands will rise to take their places!"

Already the arrival of the *kedjouronan* of Passangau, a powerful rajah who disposed of 8000 spearmen, had been announced. Allah would protect his children, and the greasy Dutch, damn them, would be tossed into the sea, friend of the Aceh, as bait for the sharks.

Frenzied cries and acclamations, akin to roaring beasts, resounded in answer to these exhortations, and above their heads the air was swarming with steel. Suddenly, a clamor arose:

"To the Three-Tiered Mountain!"

And, from every breast rose the cry of:

"To the Mountain! Allah! Allah!"

Some distance from the *kraton*, a strange monument from the era of idolatry, less distant than the Muslim conversion might suggest, had served for human sacrifices, and, since then, had been reserved for executions. Enormous egg-shaped stones formed an almost uninterrupted guard-rail around each tier, through which one could still see the evidence of past bloodshed.

The call had been heard and had given way to a general frenzy. By way of the great avenue facing the *kraton*, from the door to Pontay-Perak, along the Kroung Daroub, the crowd had rushed, lifting upon its shoulders the *panglimas* and *kedjouronans* who, brandishing their serrated *goloks*,[7] roared out their furious cries.

And when this great human wave, far more sinister than one upon the sea, passed before the *gloumpang*, a tree whose boughs resembled the spread-out plumage of

---

[7] Malaysian machete.

a bird, and beneath which General Kohler had been killed during the attack upon the mosque, there was a great explosion of howling which lost all semblance of humanity.

The race continued thrusting forward haphazardly, as if each group sought individually to reach their goal first: the Three-Tiered Mountain, the foundation of which now delineated itself above the banana, grapefruit and *koupoulos* trees, themselves dominated by the sumptuous *soukouw*, or breadfruit, its huge leaves deployed in an emerald canopy.

They had arrived; upon a signal, all voices were suddenly quieted. From the shoulders that bore them, the great leaders had been hoisted to the first tier. There, having sat upon the brilliantly white, oval stones, they remained still, eyes lowered, waiting for Allah's protection to manifest itself by some tangible sign.

There then rose from the crowd, muffled, sussurating, somewhat ill-defined, a murmur one might have thought to be issuing from the bowels of the Earth, a soft and mysterious rumbling. From all these men, lately so angry and loud, half- closed lips gave forth sounds in a barely perceptible unity. Little by little, in imperceptible steps, grew the hymn of ancient times, of when the Acehs sought to mimic the rustles and murmurs of Nature, an invocation both supplicatory and passionate to the mysterious forces occupying land and sky.

The leaders had risen, and, above this strange prayer of a thousand sighs, had cried forth in loud strident bursts the name of Allah. Suddenly, as if the Mohammedan God had decided to answer these imperious petitions, unexpectedly and almost instantaneously, the scene on the monument changed. On the second and third tiers, in every corner, between and atop every rounded stone, naked men had suddenly sprung up, brandishing blades and *assegai*,[8] creatures of fantasy evoked in a legend-inspired dream.

The Sakays! The Sakays! The wild people of the Malacca peninsula, denizens of the jungle, having little intercourse with other men, and who had, until now, remained indifferent to the battles raging in Sumatra. They had appeared out of nowhere, in great numbers, and energetic. The Aceh leaders extended their hands towards them, called to them, encouraging them to approach. A bold and combative race, the Sakay, who had swum across the straits, still appeared hesitant to give up their isolation and join their fellows.

But one of them stepped out from among them, and, clearing in one bound the span from a lower tier to that above, a jump of no less than four meters, prostrated himself before Toukou Ibrahim, *panglima* of 26 *moukims*. Raising his foot, the *panglima* placed it upon the Sakay's head to complete his act of submission.

The Sakay, who had thus prostrated himself before the *panglima*, was a horrible sight. While his companions, energetic, tall, strapping, with abundant black hair and powerful muscles, gave the impression of creatures drawing their vitality from the primary elements of Nature, this one was a monster of a sort, shrunken by human misery. Lean, skinny, with bones showing through his parchment-thin, squamous, leprous-like skin, his eyes ringed by a scarlet ridge, this specter, escaped from some diabolical haunt, nonetheless enjoyed a universal reputation within the archipelago. Of the Sakay, he was the only one to have traveled throughout Malaysia; he was said to be a sage, a sorcerer, a healer. He had power

---

[8] A light spear or javelin,

over the lightning and the rain, and he commanded a respectful terror.

The *panglima* had brought him to his feet, and now, between the two men, the Sakay and the Aceh, a low-voiced colloquy began.

Igli-Otou, such was the name of the Sakay, was animated in his speech, his emaciated arms waving about violently. The *panglima* listened attentively to him, and when the Sakay was finished, gestured to his two colleagues the *panglimas* of 22 and of 25 *moukims*.

Frightful in his ugliness, almost beautiful by excess of hideousness, Igli-Otou waited. His Sakay brothers had not moved and kept their great black eyes upon him; it was understood that it was from him, and him only, that a call to arms would be accepted.

The *panglima* of 26 *moukims*, Toukou Ibrahim, then approached the edge of the stone platform and, with an imperious gesture, commanded silence. All were quiet and Toukou Ibrahim cried out:

"Aceh brothers, our Sakay brothers come to offer us their strong arms and their courage!"

"*Menang! menang!*"[9] cried out all the voices.

"Our Sakay brothers have been pillaged by the *Ourang Oulou* [10] and their women have been taken, their children's throats slashed."

"*Talo! Talo!*"[11]

"Our Sakay brothers wish to avenge themselves; they will sacrifice their lives to punish the invaders. They come to us to fight to their last drop of blood. But, before all this, they wish the Sultan to accept one condi-

---

[9] Bravo!
[10] The Dutch (or white men).
[11] Exclamations of anger

tion, which they intend to reveal only to him. If our Lord, Sultan Mahmoud, Allah's Servant on Earth, consents to it, 2000 Sakays will join us, and together, we will drive away the invader. Igli-Otou, our Sakay brother, have I correctly stated your thoughts?"

The old man, his two hands folded on his chest, nodded in agreement.

"So," continued Toukou Ibrahim, "we will return to the *kraton* with a deputation of our Sakay brothers, and we will solicit an audience with the Sultan. All of you, be confident! Welcome in your *kampongs* [12] the Sakay who, tomorrow, will fight for you. Go, keep the peace between you and may Allah protect you!"

But a raucous cry, then a wild clamor, interrupted the proceedings. One of the Sakay, a hairy giant, whose face was entirely concealed, cheeks to forehead, beneath a thick beard, sprang before the *panglima* who was getting ready to come down, and, in a loud voice, frightening in its shrillness, shouted:

"No! Why go to the Sultan? Death to the enemy! God wishes the sacrifice! Forward! Forward!"

His wild face trembled with fury; in the excited state the crowd was in, his calls to violence did not fall on deaf ears.

"*Talo! Talo!*" now screamed the Acehs.

The Waslah leader expressed the general feeling:

"What does our Sakay brother mean? Let him explain himself! If there is an act of justice to accomplish, we are ready! Let him speak! Let him speak!"

"Aceh brothers..." began the *panglima* of 26 *moukims*.

---

[12] Homes.

But the crowd cut him off by its clamors. A few of the Sakays encircled Igli-Otou, and, given the brutality of their gestures, there was no doubt that they would have readily overthrown his authority were he not to obey their wishes.

Igli-Otou, concerned above all else with his popularity, decided to speak.

"Aceh brothers," he cried, "the God who presides over the matters of Heaven and Earth, who loves the Aceh and gives the Sakay his protection, demands, for the good of the country, that the miserable white woman, who, for five years, has soiled with her very presence the holy island of Sumatra be put to death. He does not wish the traitorous race to affront you on your own soil; he does not wish the offspring of the accursed race of men from beyond the seas to be able, while growing up in your lands, to spy upon you, betray you, and to sell you to the enemy!"

Of whom did he speak? Who, then, was this person, so dangerous that her death was demanded by the God of the Sakays? Already, the Acehs had understood, and a name came forth, in an exclamation of rage and hatred:

"Mayha! Mayha! Yes! Yes! The God of the Acehs is the God of justice! Death to Mayha the white woman! Death to the children of Mayha!"

Was it for political reasons, or purely out of pity, that Igli-Otou had not sought to accomplish an act of violence without the Sultan's assent? But his plans, whatever they had been, were now thwarted; a current of fury blew over everyone's head.

Perhaps the horrible scene they planned disturbed the three *panglimas*, but the people's anger could no longer be contained.

"Death to Mayha! Death to Mayha!"

The name was now like a war-cry. Igli-Otou, drawing the Sakays behind him, and the entire mass of people like a raging torrent, hurled down the slope that led to the shores of the Kroung-Deroub.

And, in the distance, at the door of a small straw-hut whose supports were bathed in the blue water, a delicately-formed woman stood, while, amongst the grasses, her two children played and laughed. This woman was Mayha, the white woman, the exile, the prisoner of the Acehs, who, for several years, after a series of tragic events which will be recounted later, meek and resigned, had devoted herself completely to her two children: George, barely ten, and Margaret, a clear complexioned, wonder-struck little girl.

She lived there in a hillock, extending goodwill to all, harmless certainly, and having no foreboding of the horrible peril which threatened her. And now, upon the savage call of Igli-Otou, the crowd surged to assault her miserable little shelter of lianas and branch-wood.

Mayha, that morning, had just bathed her two children: little Margaret was five now, gracious, happy and carefree, growing up in this luxuriant environment.

George was entering his tenth year of life; he was a robust, plucky young man, with pale eyes and a climate-darkened complexion. The elegant curls of his dark-brown hair framed a handsome and energetic face. Mayha had told him of the terrible events of the past; and, in the child's soul, which under the climate had already almost blossomed into that of a man, anger and desire for vengeance had grown.

Mayha tried to calm him, but could she really blame him when he cursed the dishonorable betrayal which had cost his father his life, his mother her liberty, and which chained him to this place of which he knew not the beauties, and only remembered the cruelties?

"Mother! Mother!" cried George, who, up on a grassy knoll, had seen the crowd rushing down from the Three-Tiered Mountain. "It seems like the savages are mad with rage... Where are they going? Ah! They're now engaging themselves upon the path which comes down to the river. Could they be coming here?"

"No, my son, that's impossible!" replied Mayha, whose heart nonetheless tightened under an involuntary anxiety. "Such numbers of men would not unite to attack those as feeble as us."

"Mother, listen to those shouts! They appear to be in a drunken fury and thirsting for blood! Mother, I tell you, it is we they menace."

Mayha, pale, took to her feet. Yes, she recognized the voices. She had heard those shouts before! She tried in vain to keep her cool.

Horrible forebodings shook her and she trembled, less for herself certainly, as she was resigned to any sacrifice for those dear ones, who meant everything to her, and which she loved with all the strength of her soul. But, as if reality had wished to destroy in a single stroke all her greatest illusions, such was the name which reached her, repeated by a hundred voices:

"Death to Mayha! Death to Mayha!"

Carried by the wind, the sound resounded in her ears like a peal of thunder, and George, too, had heard them. He ran to the straw-hut and grabbed a bow and arrow, for he had learned to handle this dangerous weapon, and his infallible eye meant that he never missed a target.

"No, child!" cried out Mayha. "I beg of you! Think not of fighting! Be careful! Think of Margaret!"

The little girl, scared by the noise, instinctively nestled into her mother's dress. Mayha looked about her. Fleeing was not an option. Besides the fact that reaching the bridge would entail traveling over far too great a distance without a single stop, the Acehs would soon overtake them...

To reach the straw-hut, one had to cross a light rope-bridge which linked the two shores of the river. George sprang towards it, ready to defend the passage.

But his mother called him back. This impending threat was to be faced with dignity and bravery, as a noble son of Europe who would, still, in death, give a lesson in courage to these madmen. And besides, any reasoning was superfluous! Igli-Otou, having outstripped his fellows, was the first to cross the bridge, and, with the first troop of followers, had run towards Mayha's home.

In an instant, Mayha, George, and poor little Margaret, were seized, thrown to the ground, and covered in bonds. Triumphant cries saluted this act of monstrous villainy. Already the knives were raised over their heads, but Igli-Otou spoke a few words, projected in a vibrant tone. He drew in the air, with his skeletal hand, a mysterious sign. The arms were lowered.

And the prisoners, bound and gagged, were taken along as the crowd shouted:

"To the *kraton*! To Sultan Mahmoud!"

TO-HO, LE TUEUR D'OR
Des cris de triomphe saluaient cet acte de mystérieuse lâcheté. (P. 76, col. 2.)

Triumphant cries saluted this act of monstrous villainy.

Chapter II

Who then was this Mayha, against whom such fierce hatred was unleashed?

It had happened some five years ago, during one of the first truces between the Acehs and the Dutch. After a number of indecisive battles, but which had, in reality, turned to the disadvantage of the invaders, the Malaysians had slowly and treacherously prepared the final blow.

An armistice had been agreed upon, with all the signs of a peaceful start; the Dutch boats had even been allowed to put in at Oulaylay. Some commerce had sprung up between the Europeans and the islanders who came to exchange their minerals and pelts for European glass-works and fabrics. The Dutch thought the game already won and that they would quickly gain control over commerce, but they had not counted on the cunning and hatred of the Malaysians, who thought of nothing but lulling their fears.

One night, during a dreadful storm, the Dutch ships saw themselves surrounded by Malay junks. The officers, so convinced of the peace, were mostly on land, among their families they had had brought from the Malacca peninsula.

The element of surprise was devastating: the Malay torched, then boarded the ships. Through the fire and smoke, they slit the throats of whoever was in reach. It was a frightful slaughter. Of those on land, who had also been surprised by the Aceh hordes, very few had been able to reach their ships, either by diving and swimming, or by untying a small boat from the shore, or by running onto a Malay junk and throwing its occupants into the sea.

The Dutch, lulled into a false sense of security, had found themselves unable to mount a resistance. They were forced to flee, and, as if this was not horror enough, those who had escaped and had been called back to duty by their leaders, and compelled to obey them, heard, on the cursed shores, the screams of those unfortunates whose throats were being slashed by the Acehs.

She who now bore the name Mayha, then bore the name Luisa Villiers and was the wife of a Dutch captain, of French extraction. (We are well acquainted with the fact that, during the reign of Louis XIV, many of our French countrymen took refuge in Holland during the religious persecutions.) Her husband, Wilhelm Villiers, commander of the brigantine *The Star*, was on land when the Malay attack broke out.

Luisa was with him, with their two children, and they spoke quietly of their plans for the future: the island, so beautiful, so rich, with its radiant sky and it heavenly landscapes, had filled them with wonder. Wilhelm had planned, with his wife's approval, to come and settle there. Even Wilhelm's brother, Peter Villiers, was ready to join them. He was a very talented chemist, and their description of the island's mineral wealth had so enthused him, that he had decided to leave Haarlem to come and join his brother's family.

It was in the midst of such placid times, of these dreams, that the cries of death had suddenly burst out. Wilhelm, believing it a mere brawl, one of those clashes so frequent among these noisy people, had run outside. But barely had he stepped out of the house that he was surrounded and taken along. He defended himself vigorously, calling upon the men he knew to be scattered about Oulaylay to rescue him. Having thus rallied around him a small troop, he managed to fray his way through. His duty was to run to the defense of his leaders but, it must be said, he did not yet fully understand the atrocity of the situation.

When, blinded by blood and raging mad, he reached the wooden pier beside the port, he saw the columns of flame rising into the air: they were the Europeans' boats burning. Then, the poor man tried to retrace his foot-steps, but what could courage and despair do before the fury of drunken murderers? His sailors, working as a human shield, finally found him, his head split open, thinking all they were rescuing was a corpse!

What had befallen him in this turmoil? But, espe-cially, what had been the fate of poor Luisa and the children? Shocked from a state of contentment by the appalling reality, the fires, the murders, the noble wom-an thought, before all else, of saving her children, of which the eldest, a boy named George, was five and the other, her daughter Margaret, was still at her breast.

While the wretches threw flaming torches onto the fragile boats, Luisa had fled through a back door, carry-ing Margaret, and pulling along George by the hand. What a sinister thing it was, this mother's flight through a night aglow with the red flames which devoured the city. But, Wilhelm! Where was he? What had befallen him? His wife knew him: intrepid and faithful to his duty until death; she thought he must have fallen under the blows of these madmen, in whom, with her womanly shrewdness, she had always sensed the latent hostility beneath the demonstrations of friendship.

TO-HO, LE TUEUR D'OR
La pauvre femme s'était enfuie portant Margaret, entrainant George par la main. (P. 97, col. 3.)

Luisa had fled through a back door, carrying Margaret,
and pulling along George by the hand.

And now, this hellish, hideous reality had been unleashed. By some singular felicity—if under such terrors
the word felicity can have a place—the young woman
wore a Malay dress, tied at the waist with a silk cord,
and her blonde hair was hidden beneath an Aceh bonnet.

This was a fancy which pleased her husband; the children themselves were dressed as rich natives, and this circumstance saved their lives.

As she fled, running through the crowd in this night rendered even darker by the pall of smoke hanging over the city, she slipped through unobserved, and was thus able to escape from the centre of the furnace itself, and reach the great forest which separated Oulaylay from Kota-Rajia. She plunged into those inextricable depths, unconcerned by the vicious beasts which seemed to her far less cruel than men. Besides, she no longer thought, no longer reasoned. Fever pounded in her brain. If she forced herself to continue running, it was because she had lost any sense of reality. Fear and despair make for their own drunkenness.

Doubtlessly, she had finally fallen like a lump in the tall grasses, yet having the marvelous instinct of shielding the child she held in her arms. The other had lain down beside her and exhausted, had fallen asleep.

How long had this prostration lasted? She never knew. When she regained consciousness, she found herself in a thatched Aceh cottage, surrounded by women who looked curiously, but not angrily, at her. She was unable to explain herself, not knowing the language of the country, but there exists between mothers a sort of free-masonry under which the same gestures are understood all over the world.

In this wilderness, it seemed that the horrific events which had turned Oulaylay into a bloodbath were still unknown. As she was feverish, and her weak state prevented her from moving on—and where would she have gone?—she accepted the asylum offered her by the Malay women.

Days and months went by. One day, emissaries from the *panglima* presented themselves at the village. One had heard that a white woman and her children were in the forest. The order had been given to bring them before their chief.

She obeyed and they interrogated her. She told the full truth, in a straightforward manner. Among those who assisted the *panglima*, some demanded her death and that of her children. These reptiles had to be crushed to the last, they argued. But the chief forced them to be silent and pardoned Luisa. The white woman would remain in the country, forbidden from ever leaving it. She would live as she pleased, however she could manage. They agreed to forget her, but no other favors were to be granted to her.

She asked, tried to find out what had befallen her husband. They told her that he was dead, witnesses stating they had seen him fall. She cried, pondered dying, then thought of her children, and concluded that whatever might occur, she had to live in order to protect and defend them.

They assigned her a modest grass-hut next to the river. She was intelligent and good-hearted; notwithstanding the hateful distrust attached to her, she managed to win over the trust, almost the affection, of those around her. She made herself loved by the children and respected by the men, and thus the years passed. She cultivated her field, did various work in exchange for the supplies necessary to survive. She had managed not to simply die.

The children grew up, happy, unconscious, unknowing of the past and believing in the future; but how often did their mother ponder their dreadful destiny! A single hope remained in the depths of her soul. She knew the strength of the Dutch. It was impossible that they would not seek to take revenge. Who knew if, one day, they might not come and deliver her from this prison, where she sometimes thought herself at the point of death?

Her husband! Oh! She could not but believe him dead, as alive, he surely would have found a way to find her, were it only to pass her a message... And besides, she knew him to be so valiant! Would he not have organized and led the expedition to recover his beloved and his children and take them away from the perils they faced?

Truly, she did not feel safe. Since the hostilities had resumed, she had sensed the rebirth of mistrust, suspicion and anger around her. Already, people kept their distance and, sometimes, she overheard threats. Now that she knew the Aceh language, she could discern those subtleties of pronunciation, which modified the meaning of words, lending them a tinge of irony or menace.

But what could she do? Was it not already a miracle that she had been allowed to live and keep her children? And, besides, what umbrage could she cause in even the most suspicious of them? A woman, a mother, focused entirely on her household, alone of her race, unable to find a confederate anywhere—had she even wished it—who could fear her? But one must take into account superstitions, ignorance and hatred.

And now, here were the Orang-Sakays, none of whom knew her, and to whom she surely had never done any harm. They imagined that the wartime disasters suffered by the Acehs were the work of this foreigner, this alien *inong* [13] who, notwithstanding the fact that she had been named *Mayha*, which meant " meek" and " harmless," was now accused of being a witch and of having let loose evil spirits in the land!

Nothing more was required to awake their poorly suppressed fury. Bewildered, near death, Mayha was carried off by the frenzied crowd towards the *kraton* where the most terrible tortures awaited her.

---

[13] Woman.

Chapter III

Following the Acehs' successive defeats, Sultan Mahmoud-Shah had spent his days confined in his palace-fortress' centrally-located funereal chapel, which housed the remains of his predecessors.

He felt his power slipping away and believed himself to be surrounded with traitors. Wily and defiant, he only maintained intimate contact with his favorite Sultana and a few chieftains whose devotion had been tested, and amongst whom he felt particularly safe, given that he held power over their lives. For days on end, he remained motionless, seated on the floor, leaning against one of the tombs, chewing on betel-nut, his face never losing its complete impassibility.

The messengers and officers sent by the *panglimas* found him there. As terrible as was the news they brought, Mahmoud-Shah showed neither the least shudder, nor the least flicker of his eyelids. At times, one might have thought him a stone idol. But beneath this apparent coolness, a savage fury brewed.

Leader, Sultan, Lord, the man remembered the time when, master of land and sea, he and his men ruthlessly ransomed and pillaged all those who had the audacity to adventure themselves along the Sumatran coasts. Angered by the daily worsening decline in his race's fortunes, he also shared the Malays' open and atavistic hatred towards the white man.

The Sultan was continually attended upon by a slave, bared saber in hand. Upon a number of occasions, upon a sign from the master, this executioner would, in a single stroke, sever the head of an inopportune counselor who had dared speak of compromise with the Dutch. The man who had brought the news of the defeat at Samalaggan had been drawn and quartered.

Combining the ancestral savagery of the Aceh with a perverted and depraved soul's refinements in cruelty, Mahmoud-Shah was a monster, feared by all and whose name always inspired dread; yet his subjects idolized him. Guilty of many heinous atrocities and crimes, he cowered in his *kraton* like a hunted beast.

He entertained strange fantasies; he kept a huge menagerie in his palace, and sought to satiate his blood-lust upon the jungle beasts. He would lock up a tiger in a narrow steel cage, the bars of which were so strong as to defy any attack, and, from outside, cravenly, he would enjoy himself torturing the animal with long metal-barbed poles, or with steel rods heated to redness in the fire. The beast screeched and roared, struggled fiercely under the grip of pain. He, silent, struck again and smiled, holding back the blows to prolong the agony.

A recent acquisition greatly interested him.

In the middle of the island, upon the mountainous ridges of a tormented landscape—all chasms and cliffs--- grew a thick jungle, which Nature, fruitful and free, had rendered impenetrable. Vines, prodigious tree-trunks, branches woven into limbs of steel, served to resist human invasion. The few who had penetrated these solitudes, and had lived to talk of it, had, since time immemorial, brought back rumors that this impregnable fortress housed a strange and frightening race of mysterious beings, more than apes, but not yet men.

They bore themselves upright, holding their head up, knew a few simple skills, but not how to make fire. According to the incoherent tales brought back by the terror-stricken travelers, these advanced ape-men had a spoken language, but one incomprehensible to any human ear. Full of vigor, they seemed peaceful, living communally in tribes in the few clearings; they even sheltered themselves from the weather inside wooden huts.

Mahmoud had promised a huge sum—5000 *ringguits*—to anyone who could lay their hands on one of these mysterious beings, and bring it to him alive and in captivity. But they appeared to be both physically invulnerable and impossible to capture by surprise. All the ambushes and traps which had been set had been in vain; only once, had an ape-man been killed, and the killer had dragged his carcass to the *kraton*.

Dead, the creature was, *in fine*, just an exceptionally large ape, some kind of gorilla. The Aceh's scientific knowledge was far too limited for anyone among them to observe the anatomical characteristics which would have established a closer link between this animal and humans.

Furious at his own discomfiture, Mahmoud had had the poor man, who had clearly misunderstood his intentions, buried alive. To complete the horror, he had tied the beast's corpse to the man's body so they could rot together.

A short time thereafter—quite recently—barely eight days ago—a troop of Aceh, returning from a battle with the Dutch, had surprised, before the very gates of Kota-Rajia, one of these fantastic creatures. He stood still, behind the last huts of the *kampong*, attentive, seemingly watching, in a state of such undivided attention that the Aceh had been able to surround him, throw themselves upon him and cover him in bonds before he could defend himself.

Nevertheless, he had fought with desperate courage; his strength was such that it had taken 20 men to subdue him. Finally, his chest struck by a saber-blow, which laid it open, he fell, and, with triumphant cries, his aggressors had taken him and delivered him to the Sultan.

His wound, as deep as it was, had healed in two days. Iron fetters were placed about his neck, on his arms and legs. When it was clear that, notwithstanding his great strength, he had been rendered powerless, he was brought before Mahmoud-Shah. Besides, the creature seems resigned to his fate and no longer resisted.

The Sultan's dream had finally come true: he beheld before him a man of the forest, one of the fantastic creatures which he so wished to investigate. The man-ape and the potentate faced each other. The latter was short, slender and monkey-like; the former towered over six feet, and was wide-shouldered, its flat chest rippling with muscles, its legs exhibiting a well-defined musculature. However, the creature's knee-cap was located on the inside, his feet were wide, and the big toe elongated and distinctly separate from the remaining toes. The great arms ended in huge hands, which reached to the knee.

However, that which characterized the mysterious being, which gave him an appearance both strange and fearsome, was his face. The head stood atop a muscular neck, very slightly tipped forward. As with the rest of the body, the skin was a downy black. On the bulging egg-shaped skull, dark hair was separated into two long strands running under the ears to the nape of the neck where they were knotted. He was entirely naked.

The forehead was ridged, protruding, the nose very wide, with up-turned nostrils, beneath which projected a mouth whose upper lip ran over edgeless, chiseled lips.

The rectilinear jaw occupied the full width of the face, giving the impression of a steel jaw. This bestial figure would have, at first glance, been indistinguishable from any other ape, was there not among all that ugliness, the compelling glimmer of those marvelous eyes.

The eyelids were large, heavy, but the eyeball protruding, the sclerotic very white, forming a circle around a continually expanding and contracting pupil, seemingly intimately linked to the creature's mode of existence. These eyes had an indefinably expectant, curious and attentive expression. So much did the animal's physiognomy differ from that of an ape, that Mahmoud had instinctively spoken to him as a man, as he would to a slave.

"Monster," he cried out to him, "who are you? From whence have you come? Are you not bold to be lurking about the homes of men? Answer, brute! Know that I am powerful among the powerful, and that your sad carcass is at my mercy. Are you deaf? Are you dumb?"

The creature did not move, not a muscle in his face even twitched. It seemed as if the Sultan's voice had never reached him. Nevertheless, one who would have observed him closely, would have seen a flash beneath his heavy-lidded, half-shut eyes, and observed his tightly fettered hands quiver.

"Lord," said one of the soldiers prostrating himself, "this animal is not deaf, for when we surprised him, he jumped upon us, having heard, albeit too late, the sound of our footsteps. He is not dumb! For when we first grappled with him, he cried out in a manner that resembled words. I swear he knows how to speak."

"Very well," said the Sultan. "Have him beaten."

They laid hold of the creature, stretched him out and tied him face-down to a plank. His bonds sank into his flesh and the iron shackles were rimmed in blood. An Ourang-Rautay—a convict—was brought forth and was ordered to strike him with a nail-studded length of bamboo. The improvised torturer took up the long rod, making it whistle through the air and waited for a signal, which was immediately given. The steel-barbed bamboo came down upon the prisoner.

Fifty blows! It was horrible. The Aceh's plaintive, agonized, closed-mouthed chant imposed its rhythm to the torture. As the creature had not let out a cry, had not even budged, one might have wondered if his flesh and muscles were molded of the same clay as man. Mahmoud thought him dead, and called out for the man to stop.

Displeased at having his victim escape him so quickly, he had the creature untied and raised upright. Blood streaming, dark red on dark skin, the creature remained standing, looking before him into his tormentor's eyes before him with a glimmer of surprise and contempt. Under that withering look, Mahmoud flinched involuntarily, and ordered the man-ape be put aside. He would be kept chained in an iron cage. The Sultan would decide later what he wished done.

After that, Mahmoud daily made his way through the *kraton* to the cell where the creature was tied up, and, assuring himself that none eavesdropped, spoke to him, at times in a voice of authority, at others in a pleading tone. The mystery surrounding this creature frightened him. Under the half-animal, half-human envelope, he sensed something horrifying, one of Nature's darkest secrets!

At such times, it would have taken little for him to have prostrated himself before the incomprehensible creature, and begged it to afford him its protection. But at other times, furious at this impassiveness that bordered on disdain, exasperated by the inflexibility of the stare and its subtle glimmer, which nonetheless remained unfaltering, he lost his composure in an insane rage.

He would then call for his weapons, blades and sticks, with which he would strike and lacerate his prisoner. But the latter would not cry out, and continued to merely watch him.

"Speak! Speak," shouted the Sultan at him. "I believe, I know that you are a man! You have secrets I want to know... Oh! I will surely force you to reveal them to me! Close your eyes! I do not wish you to look at me so!"

And yet, he could not build up the resolve to destroy those eyes, whose dull look weighed so heavily upon him. It seemed to him that doing so would constitute a sacrilege. Days came and went. Mahmoud tried to conquer the ape-man through starvation. He ordered that he be given nothing to eat. The creature refused all meat anyway, accepting only bananas or *soukoun*.[14] He was not given any for three days. Then, in the narrow space he was allowed, he squatted, his legs folded beneath him. He had not budged, moaned, or spoken any more than before; only now, in the white of his eyes, the look was more acute, more daring, an unfathomable reflection of reproach and anger. Tired of this battle, but still wishing to defeat what he thought was brutish stubbornness, Mahmoud-Shah had had the creature untied, and had ordered it relieved of its shackles.

---

[14] Breadfruit.

Keeping no more than an iron grillwork between them, he had had him brought into the tomb of the Sultans, and there, for long hours, he spoke to him, gesticulated at him, tried to bring him to some sudden outburst. Sometimes, he thought he could see that the creature—ape-like—was on the brink of becoming human; he knew himself to be understood; the eyes had a surprising involuntary eloquence that inflamed all the more his desire to triumph over this resistance.

It was at one such moment that, after a sudden knock at the door of the sanctuary, one of his top dignitaries, the *panglima* of 22 *moukims*, entered.

"What do you want?" shouted the Sultan. "What is this audacity that allows you to violate my solitude?"

"Lord", replied the *panglima* as he prostrated himself, "important events are now taking place, which could have the most fortunate of influences upon upcoming events. The Orang-Sakay have come forth from their forests and have offered us their courage and devotion."

"The Sakay!" exclaimed the Sultan. "Those wretched nomads that rank beneath the vilest of beasts..."

"But, Lord, they are many, and their hatred towards the white man is great. The Dutch, damn them, have entered their forests and killed some of their friends. They aspire to vengeance. They are precious auxiliaries who will give up their lives for the salvation of the Malay nation... Lord, please, do not reject them!

"Every day, the enemy advances. The ring which besieges us tightens and our brothers fall beneath its blows. Our Sakay brothers in their sampans and junks will attack them along the coast, while we will push them from the interior, our spears at their back. Thus will our ancient state of Perak recover its freedom, and with it, its riches... O Lord, heed the voice of your *pan-glimas*... Accept an alliance with the Orang-Sakay."

Mahmoud had fallen back on his pillows, thinking. He had, firmly anchored in his heart, hatred and contempt for the Sakay, whom he judged to be an inferior race. However, he knew that his *panglima* spoke the truth. Their courage, built on savagery, could serve as useful support...

Involuntarily, he shifted his eyes to the strange creature which seemed to listen attentively to what was being said, although, obviously, he could not understand the language. It seemed to him that a grin had appeared upon those silent features. Could the creature be contemplating the dangers to which the Aceh would expose themselves if they refused the help that could save them? Was the ape-man, deep in his heart, laughing? Mahmoud came to the sudden realization that he had no more certain enemy than his prisoner, his nemesis... His gaze fixed upon him, he said: "*Panglima*, I heed your wise counsel. Have the Sakay leaders brought before me."

"O Lord, that is not all! I pray thee, listen to the end of my report. The Orang-Sakay have left their solitudes for no other reason than to avenge themselves, and in their hatred of the white man, they demand a token proof that the Aceh also bear such a hatred."

"A proof! What? Do these wretches dare impose conditions?"

The *panglima* lowered his voice:

"There are times when caution is the best policy. Let us first profit from the support they offer us, and then, later, we can think of curing our temporary allies of their preposterous pride!"

"So be it! What do they want then?"

"Lord, by your generous boon, we have allowed a white woman and her two children to live in a hut by the river. This woman is a witch who casts evil spells on our people. Igli-Otou, the Sakay prophet, has proof of her perversity, and he demands that this woman and her children be put to death!"

The Sultan made a scornful gesture, saying:

"What do I care about them! Kill them!"

"Lord, the people want you to pronounce the sentence yourself."

"I will do it. Have the wretch brought before me. Ah! By Allah! I feel like meting out some justice..." and he added, turning towards the ape-man: "And it pleases me to have you see me exert my power of life and death."

Upon a signal, the doors opened and the Sakay chieftains entered, led by the horrible Igli-Otou, followed by the Aceh chieftains, and behind them, the crowd who prostrated themselves on the threshold.

Then, the soldiers thrust forward Mayha and her two children.

Chapter IV

During this frantic race, which had taken her and her children through the city, the unfortunate Mayha had suffered twofold, both from the bonds which held her delicate limbs, and from the horrible thoughts which had suddenly come to her mind. She had lived in such a peaceful manner, almost happy, having sacrificed her past.

TO-HO, LE TUEUR D'OR

Pendant cette course forcenée à travers la ville, d'horribles pensées s'imposaient à son esprit. (P. 129. col. 1.)

During this frantic race through the city, horrible thoughts had suddenly come to mind.

She had ended up becoming interested in these Aceh which surrounded her, almost loving them, lavishing her attention upon them, teaching them all sorts of things about life and asking only in return a bit of sympathy for her children.

What a rude awakening! It seemed that she had lived in the whirlpool of a hideous nightmare. George! Margaret! Was it indeed true that they were in the hands of these furious men, these savage brutes who battered them? In vain, she tried to keep her cool; in vain, she tried to reason, to grasp within her troubled thoughts some reason to hope!

No, this was death, brutal and atrocious, a thunderbolt falling upon the innocent. Suddenly, she found herself standing in the magnificent and sinister mausoleum of the ancient Aceh Sultans, her two children by her side who, pale and weak, could barely keep from collapsing to the marble-tiled floor.

She sensed that the man with the jewel-encrusted clothing, surrounded by guards with bare sabers in hand, was the leader, Sultan Mahmoud-Shah who, not long ago, had fomented the traitorous revolt in which her husband, the father of her children, had died. On his scraggly, tanned face, she read a brutality so revolting that all her blood surged back to her heart.

It was upon this monster—of whose heinous crimes she had heard—that the fate of her children depended. But, at the same time, as a greater horror invaded her soul, the peril became more immediate, embodied in this man who held the power of life or death. She shook these feelings and pulled herself together.

She was a woman, she was European, she was a mother. Her duty, her dignity, her motherly love demanded that she fight to the bitter end. Women have these bouts of heroic nerve that galvanize them completely. However, in the mausoleum's tall chamber, to which the steles of the dead lent their pale and sepulchral tones, under a light that filtered down through narrow windows set in the ceiling, a deep silence had established itself. An etiquette of submission and respect had returned it to its past glories.

For the crowd, pressed against the doors, the Sultan was Allah's Servant on Earth; they didn't see him as he was, a small-minded, squat, gnome-like man, but rather transfigured through divine and human omnipotence. As if struck with bewilderment, the Aceh remained prostrated, forehead to the ground. The *panglimas* kneeled.

The Sakays alone—and Igli Otou—had contented themselves to bow deeply. These sons of sylvan freedom had an insolence borne of their solitude. Besides, Igli-Otou and the Sultan were not strangers to each other, and a leaven of hatred that struggled to be contained, existed between them. The few people that noticed, behind the Sultan, separated from him by iron grillwork, a huge, simian form, shuddered, and wondered if this was not some infernal genie. It stood erect, hanging by the whitish extremities of its fingers, which stuck out through the mesh of the grillwork, its eyes opened wide, its huge head cocked and thrust forward attentively.

The Sultan, with a sign, invited Igli-Otou to state his request, and the Sakay sorcerer, with the grandiloquence of official orators, presented the demands of his people. They were ready to devote themselves to the independence of the Malay people. They brought their courage and energy with sincerity. Furthermore, Antou, their god, would provide them with its omnipotent aid. But, was it natural or logical that the Aceh protect, defend and maintain within its own bosom a ruthless enemy of its race? Had it been that this woman was alone, one might have allowed that she was harmless. But her children were growing, and they represented for all true believers, for the liberty of the Aceh, of the Sakay, and of the Battaks, a living threat. Antou, the god of the Sakays, had warned his faithful people of this unavoidable peril, nay, perhaps even fatal peril, and his voice had been heard by the Sakay.

Yes, they would fight alongside their Aceh brothers, they would not haggle over the cost of their lives, and none would rest until the white man was forever expelled from the sacred soil of Sumatra, but what they demanded before any of this, was the death of the witch, and the death of her children.

Igli-Otou concluded:

"The hunter does not leave behind the tigress and her cubs."

A clamor saluted the Sakay's last words. Crowds, be they civilized or savage, are as prone to suggestions of hate and brutality. The *panglima*, with one gesture, ordered silence, then, speaking in turn, he supported Igli-Otou's demand.

This woman—much testimony proved it—had maintained her race's instinct for treachery and vengeance. The few defeats the Aceh had endured were due to her, to the conjurations and diabolical ceremonies she performed, to the infernal rites she practiced on the darkest nights.

Suddenly, loudly, Mayha interrupted him:

"Sultan," she cried, "Lord of the believers, this man lies! He knows that all his information is false. That I be accused by the Sakay, I could always forgive and impute to their ignorance, but this man is a criminal, who prefers lies, knowing full well his words are slanderous."

"Enough! Silence! Put her to death!" cried out a hundred voices in the crowd.

Mayha, standing proudly, radiant in her energetic resistance, crossed her arms, looked at the Sultan in the face, and again proclaimed:

"These men are mad. Lord, in the name of truth, in the name of justice, I adjure you to listen to me."

The Sultan remained impassive; it seemed that not one of these voices reached him, neither that of the supplicant, not that of the people.

Igli-Otou, exasperated, had taken up his testimony. Strengthened by the support he received from the *panglima* and the savage crowd, he raised his voice higher, insisting particularly on the death of the children, tomorrow's traitors.

Once again, Mayha fought back.

"Lord, Lord," she cried to the Sultan, "what these men are proposing to you is a disgraceful crime! Was their fury only directed at me, I would not even protest. You could have killed me long ago, but you did not, you let me live! And this life which you spared, while killing my husband, you can take it back. Of what am I guilty? I do not know. But against me, against me only, I admit all and renounce even to plead my case.

"But my children! My poor little George, so good, so gentle, so ignorant of human wickedness! My dear weak little Margaret, barely weaned from my breast! You dare to claim them as your enemies, as threats to your independence? Lord! Lord! Look at them, deign lower your eyes upon these weak and innocent creatures! Who would dare accuse them?

"If you must have a victim, I am here, I the European, I the white woman, the one you despise as not of your race, but out of mercy, out of pity, out of justice, in

46

the name of the God you worship, in the name Allah the All-Knowing and Merciful, I beg you to strike me down, but spare my children!"

Mayha spoke the Aceh tongue fluently, even eloquently, and notwithstanding her European accent, her speech was understood by the crowd, in which there were women and mothers. Certain feelings now began to trouble these rough rather than truly wicked natures, and a woman's voice even cried out:

"She is right! Spare the children!"

But Igli-Otou, sensing the danger, took up yet more vehemently and cruelly his testimony:

"Are not the Aceh children as worthy as those of this European? Did the Aceh mothers not bewail the death of their sons, butchered by the white man? Did they not suffer, more than any, the ferocity of the accursed invaders? Did they not burn Pallak, the flourishing *kampong*, where women and children all perished in the flames? Did they not massacre the entire population of Sidjoh, and were there not children there? The Sakay god demands a sacrifice—who would dare refuse him? Besides, were the Aceh opposed to what is asked of them, the thousand Sakay will depart for fear of being exposed to the spells of that abominable she-demon and of her impure offspring!"

He had hit the right note. This evocation of horrible events, wherein the fury of the whites had manifested itself in all its horror, was more powerful than any appeal to mercy. The cries for death resounded more loudly, more authoritatively.

The Sultan raised his hand, drew himself up. All were silent. It was the decisive moment. In a muffled voice, Mahmoud-Shah spoke:

"My Sakay sons," he said, "Children of Allah, welcome to thee! Fight the good fight with us against our eternal enemy, the greedy and ferocious Dutchmen. Our ranks are open to you, and you shall take your place amongst the defenders of Aceh. We have weighed, in our wisdom, the demands which you put to us, remembering that a free people must not give asylum to the enemies of the state."

Here he stopped, and made a sign to his guards, who went to Mayha, whom they seized and dragged before him. The two children followed, trembling, hanging on to her dress.

"Woman," continued Mahmoud, "you are convicted of having, though your spells, brought disaster and ruin to the land of Allah—what do you have to say in your defense?"

Mayha tried in vain to regain her composure; the Sakay sorcerer's vile testimony had overwhelmed her. What could one say to such absurd accusations whose inanity she felt it was impossible to prove? The Sultan's question brutally summed up these absurd calumnies. She could only deny them. She did so:

"I never hurt anyone," she said softly, "and on the contrary, tried to accomplish all the good that was in my power to do."

"Will you deny that you are with our enemies in spirit?"

"I am of the white race. My husband, the father of my children, was killed by the Aceh, yet never a word of anger came from my lips. I may not have forgotten, but from the depths of my souls, I have forgiven!"

And, drawing against her the two children, which she wrapped in her arms, she continued:

"Most powerful Lord, I am but a poor, powerless, defenseless woman. Who then could fear me? Or be afraid of these little beings who know not of anger and hatred?"

But a grumbling interrupted her speech; the crowd was getting restless. What good were such hesitations, what good were such pleadings? To death! To death!

The Sakay sorcerer took a step towards the Sultan:

"Son of Allah!" he cried out, "beware the golden tongue and the hypocritical words! This woman was seen at night devoting herself to infernal ceremonies."

"Yes! Yes!" shouted some voices.

"It is not true!" cried out the poor woman.

"And the children were with her, helping her in her diabolical conjurations!"

"A lie! All of this is lies! Ah! miserable Sakay," she said, rising and staring at Igli-Otou in the face, "why do you accuse me? What harm have I inflicted upon you? You know well that, of all these words you speak, not one is not an odious slander."

In a sharp voice, Igli-Otou replied:

"In the name of the Orang-Sakay, I demand the death of this woman and her children. Otherwise, we will return to our canoes and will return to the depths of our forest, where we will know well how to evade our enemies' strikes. Sakay brothers, have I spoken well?"

"Yes! Yes!" cried out the Sakay, brandishing their weapons, which glittered with a sinister glint in the prevailing twilight.

The *panglima* of the 22 *moukims* said aloud:

"The salvation of the Aceh people is the supreme law. Sultan Mahmoud, render justice!"

"So be it!" said Mahmoud. "Let it be done according to your wishes. I give you this woman and her children, that they be taken to the great Toko Square and put to death before the people."

"Good! Good!" cried out all the voices.

Mayha heard; she rushed towards the Sultan, slipping from the hands that wished to hold her back, and she cried, and begged, trying to grab his clothing, saying:

"All powerful Lord! Mercy! Not for me, but for my poor little children! If it is a crime to be of the white race, they are innocent of it, as how can it be a crime to be born? Sultan, Sultan, I give myself up, let me be killed, let me be tortured, let me be torn limb from limb, but have mercy on them!"

As she spoke, her throat torn by her desperate cries, she saw the mysterious creature, the unheard of ape-man, standing up in the cage, behind the Sultan, its fingers gripping the mesh, watching wide-eyed this scene of desperation. Did he understand? Had he the slightest notion of the iniquity that was being perpetrated? His jaws snapped and his face contorted itself.

"Ah!" cried out Mayha, driven to distraction by the Sultan's silence, "I know not what this monstrous beast is, but I am certain he would show greater pity than a man!"

There was a dull rumbling. The ape-man shook the bars of his cage, but without paying any attention to him, Mahmoud-Shah said, in an annoyed tone:

"Let this woman and her children be taken away! I have spoken!"

Igli-Otou ran to her and placed his hand on her shoulder. She turned, saw his hideous face, and, in a paroxysm of despair, shoved her hands in his face to push him away. But the Orang-Sakay threw themselves upon her, upon her children—it was the end, death had come!

At this very moment, there rang out a loud, anxious, bugle-call.

The doors of the mausoleum opened suddenly and an Aceh chief appeared. He made his way through the crowd, and cried out:

"Sultan Mahmoud, the Dutch are sending a man to parley."

The Sultan knew that it was not the first time that, to fulfill their mission, those sent by the invaders had had the courage to come to the heart of the Aceh, bearing the Europeans' messages. Not one had ever returned.

"Let no one leave!" cried the Sultan. "Brother Sakay, sons of Aceh, remain. Battaks and Yolos, Children of Allah, close up your ranks around me, your supreme leader, and we shall answer the enemy's insolent envoy as is proper."

The alarm was such that the attention of the crowd had suddenly been diverted from Mayha and her children; besides, the celebration of their deaths could be put off. The three victims were closely confined in a corner of the great room and guarded by the Sakay. Mayha, in her shattered emotional state, lay sprawled on the ground, her two children desperately clinging to her. A complete silence fell.

A tall, blindfolded Dutch officer appeared on the threshold.

Chapter V

A deep silence reigned within the mausoleum which served as Sultan Mahmoud-Shah's state-room. Suddenly, all voices were quelled, and, while not spoken, the hatred and enmity felt towards the outsider and enemy were only more ardent. From the eyes of the Aceh, particularly those of the women, it flashed towards the soldier. Straight as a board, head up, pacing firmly, unhesitatingly yet without braggadocio, he followed between the Aceh guards, without seeing where he was being taken.

A large area had been cleared before the throne, upon which the Sultan was sitting in a quasi-hieratic pose. The Dutchman, judging by the decorations on his uniform, held the rank of ship's captain. He was a man of 40 or so. He was placed in the middle of a half-circle whose circumference was guarded by Aceh and Orang-Sakay soldiers. Then, the doors of the mausoleum were closed again.

In the cage, the ape-man was standing still and watching.

The Sultan gave an order and the blindfold was taken from the officer's forehead. He looked around calmly. The *panglima* of 22 *moukims* stood beside Mahmoud, as it devolved to him to question the Dutchman.

"Officer," he said, "what brings you here. You presented yourself to one of our outposts and asked to be brought before our most serene Sultan, our Lord, submitting yourself to any conditions which would be imposed. Your wish has been granted. Enemy of our country, you are in the midst of those you persecute. You stand before the Lord, Son of Allah. Speak."

The officer bowed respectfully before Mahmoud, and, straightening up, said:

"In the name of my Lord, the King of Holland, represented in this country by Colonel van der Hyeden, I, ship's captain, spokesman, claiming my right to free speech, I bring you, Sultan Mahmoud-Shah, and you all, inhabitants of the island of Sumatra, those propositions which are made to you and upon which the future holds. Are you prepared to listen to me?"

"Speak," said the *panglima*.

"I have nothing to impart to you that you don't already know. Our weapons have overwhelmed your brave resistance, and while praising your courage, I must not hide the fact that all hope is lost for you. Our vessels have retaken the port of Oulaylay and have successfully blockaded the coast. At Deli, we have captured your arsenals and a large corps of Battaks was forced to surrender. Finally, the victory at Samalaggan has made us masters of all the regions north of Kota-Rajia. You are surrounded by an ever-tightening circle of steel and fire. Our troops await only a signal to mount a decisive assault on this *kraton*, your last fortress. You are courageous, you are strong, but against the strength of the European armies, all your efforts would be in vain and would only result in a pointless massacre.

"Enough blood has already flowed; enough catastrophes have befallen your poor country. In the name of reason, in the name of humanity, I come, on my master's orders, to ask you to end this deadly struggle, the outcome of which is no longer in question. Instead, we offer you peace."

"Uunder what conditions?" said the *panglima* in a voice trembling with anger.

"Your people, your properties, your religion, your customs, your women will be respected. Your soldiers will leave the *kraton* and give up their arms. All the redoubts, forts, and public buildings will be turned over to the protection of the Dutch. You, Sultan Mahmoud, shall be deemed sacred and our troops will answer for your security. You will be at liberty to discuss the conditions of your surrender with our leader."

"That is to say," said the *panglima*, "that you come here proposing to soldiers, patriots, men who have guns and feel themselves to be free, that they commit the vilest of cowardice?"

"I am a soldier," replied the Dutchman, "and I know better than anyone that the necessities of war are cruel, but the more valiantly one has fought, the more honorably one can accept defeat. If you accept the proposals that I bring you, your honor will be intact and your independence guaranteed under a European protectorate; if you stubbornly continue a fight—which I assure you, without bragging, would doom you to defeat—before the Sun sets, our shells will destroy your homes, your palaces and your mosques; steel and fire will open the way for us, and our troops will complete their work of conquest.

"Sultan Mahmoud! It is to your justice, to your humanity, that I make this appeal. There is still time to spare your people from the horrible experiences of a last battle in which so many lives will be pointlessly sacrificed. Give your assent to an immediate capitulation, one which will be honorable and which, I pledge in the name of my master, will not hurt your feelings of righteous pride. Europeans will then enter no longer as enemies, but as friends and protectors."

As he spoke, without raising his voice, in an even and firm tone, a fever appeared to possess all the listeners. They did not interrupt him, but their looks, their gestures, their hands worrying about their weapons, the twitching of their limbs, all pointed to their growing rage being ready to explode.

But the one who was least able to control himself was the Sultan.

Unmindful of his dignity, he leapt to his feet, and, arming himself with a nearby saber, he ran to the officer and struck him full on the forehead, shouting:

"Dog! How dare you insult me with your disgraceful proposals? Die then!—and so all those who dare insult the noble Aceh."

In an instinctive gesture, the officer had turned aside the weapon, which glanced off his skull, scraping along his skin. Blood came forth from the wound. He cried out:

"This is a most cowardly act! I am here as a peace envoy, protected by sacred law. You have no right to lay a hand on me!"

The *panglimas* threw themselves before the Sultan and were barely able to contain him. They were displeased to see the Son of Allah lower himself to taking on an executioner's role.

"You who listen to me!" continued the officer, whose bloodied face was a terrible sight, "already, in the past, you have killed my wife and children! Are you nothing but a race of assassins?"

At that moment, a high pitched, heart-rending cry rang out. Parting the Sakay ranks, who, in their keen interest in the scene, had somewhat relaxed their vigilance,

Mayha, pale and disheveled, ran to the officer and threw herself in his arms, shouting:

"Wilhelm! My Wilhelm! You're alive! O save me! Save your children!"

"Luisa!" the officer cried out in turn, hugging her to his chest. Thus, in the past, had the husband believed his wife and his dear children to have been massacred; and so she had been convinced that the same fate had happened to him. But now, they were reunited after so many years, in yet an even more tragic circumstance.

At first, Mayha, dispirited, broken, had not paid any attention to the scene which was going on. Her mind distracted, sluggish, she had barely heard the words which were spoken. Then, all of a sudden, she seemed to recognize the voice that was speaking; she had given ear to it and, suddenly, when the officer, overcome with despair, had spoken these words: "My wife, my children!" she had woken from her torpid state as from an electric shock.

The impossible might be true! The dead had risen from their tombs! And now, both of them were clasped in each other's arms, in the middle of this hostile, maddened crowd which roared like a host of wild beasts. The *panglima* of the 22 *moukims* was trying in vain to calm the crowd down. Igli-Otou, the madman, cried out:

"To the Toko! To the Toko! All of you! The man, the woman, the children! Sakay, Aceh, avenge yourselves and make Antou look upon us with favor ! Death to them! Death!"

At his barking voice, which rang out like a bugle, a rush started in the previously hesitant masses. In the blink of an eye, Wilhelm, Mayha, who, for the first time in years, had rediscovered her true name—Luisa—the tiny George and poor Margaret, whose weaponless father could not even attempt to defend, were grabbed and taken away towards the execution grounds on the Toko plaza, littered with low-set huts, stores and tents. In an instant, the mausoleum was empty, the Sultan himself having been drawn along with the crowd towards the plaza.

None had considered the ape-man who was still in his cage, behind the metal grillwork. He then arched his back, braced his arms against the steel bars, and, in a superhuman effort, his enormous muscles tightened. The bars, bending under this astonishing force, twisted and broke. An opening was made.

But the creature was large, his shoulders wide, his chest colossal. Nonetheless, he managed to slip out, bruising himself, tearing his skin and drawing blood, but this did not prevent him from pushing his frame up against the steel and forcing it to spread apart. He found himself outside, standing in the middle of the stones which marked the tombs of the Sultans. For a moment, he paused before these gold-inlaid and jewel-incrusted markers, as if pondering something. He also looked around, curiously, as if hypnotized by the gold and ruby-laden oriental ornamentation. Then, he shook his head, reached the door, which the crowd had left open, and slipped through the trees behind the straw huts, crawling or jumping, moving forward.

Meanwhile, the Orang-Sakay, satisfied at last to have their hands on their victims, dragged them along to the execution grounds. They arrived, and, in the middle of a quickly improvised circle, the two Europeans and their children were grouped together, waiting for the final blow.

A short deliberation occurred: a huge Sakay, bearing a two-handed saber, was to fill the office of executioner. The crowd was howling with impatience. Why such a delay? Why had one not been stuck down yet? Why could the people not yet throw themselves upon the corpses and fight it out for a bloody trophy?

Two of the *panglimas* had approached Igli-Otou and were involved in a heated discussion. Evidently, they were proposing something which he refused to accept. But the Aceh leaders, joining the *panglimas*, were addressing themselves to the Sakay chiefs, trying to convince them—but of what?

It was this: less naive than the crowd, the *panglimas* had understood that the words of the European were no mere bluster. What he had said was true: the Dutch would, under the protection of their artillery, deliver a furious assault upon the city, and, as valiant as the defenders of Koto-Rajia might prove, the outcome of the battle was not in doubt.

But a way of turning this defeat into a victory presented itself. A number of things come about by happenstance. The dramatic recognition of husband and wife, of father and children, exposed a situation from which a marvelous, foolproof advantage could be taken: it was a gift from God to the besieged—why throw it away? And the *panglimas* finally won their point. Igli-Otou allowed himself to be convinced and, strong in his undisputed authority, he quelled the crowd's impatience and restlessness. Then, Toukou Polim, *panglima* of the 22 *moukims*, approached the Dutch officer, Wilhelm Villiers.

The latter, prepared for death, had had to a final exchange with his beloved Luisa, in which they had expressed all the emotions of their past, remembered their former happiness, their trials, and their sufferings. In a few words, they exchanged thoughts which encompassed years. The mother, forgetful of the peril, held little Margaret, who—as such mercies are afforded to infants—was asleep. George, pale, already understanding, but putting on a good face, held his father's hand and gazed upon him with loving eyes.

"Captain," said Toukou Polim, "will you allow me a moment to talk to you."

Wilhelm's smile was full of irony.

"There is nothing I can refuse you," he said. "What do you wish from me?"

Then, taking him aside and speaking in a low and hurried voice, Toukou Polim explained to him that he was lost: his death, that of his wife and children, was only minutes away; yet, he could save himself and those he loved.

The Dutchman looked attentively upon this tanned and wrinkled face, on which one could only read wiliness and lies.

"What must I do for that?" he asked.

"Return to your camp and announce that we will offer our submission."

The officer, momentarily perplexed, looked at him in surprise.

"Let the Dutch enter our city, not as enemies, but as friends, as you yourself stated; let your leaders come first to discuss the terms of our capitulation; let your sailors come amongst us confident, not as soldiers ready for carnage, but as brothers. We wish to deal in particular with Colonel van der Heyden—personally. Persuade him to come here as an ally, a protector, with an escort that represents neither a provocation nor a threat—such is the mission we offer you, Captain, and should you accept it, you will be freed."

Wilhelm now understood: what they were proposing was simply a shameful betrayal, to draw the Colonel and the top officers of the Dutch army into an ambush. The long-ago massacre, from which he had miraculously escaped, would occur all over again. However, he pretended to not have caught his interlocutor's lies.

"What of my wife and my children?" he asked.

"You will agree that it is fair that we keep them as hostages. If you promise to bring us the Colonel and his entourage, under peaceful conditions, and have not deceived us, we will honor our promise and free them too. However, if unlike what we have agreed upon, your countrymen arrive here as enemies..."

"You would cut the throats of those hostages. Well! Noble *panglima*, know that a European officer is not and cannot be your dupe. You're asking me no more and no less than to deliver my leaders into your hands. This would be both stupid and a crime. I will not buy our lives at that price."

"Ah! Be careful! Just a sign from me and the executioner will have the better of your insolence."

"I don't doubt it; however, noble lord, will you hear me out? Time marches on, and it was arranged with my superiors that, if I did not return within two hours of my point of entrance into Kota-Rajia, the attack would proceed. These two hours are up. In turn, since I am not dead yet, I call upon you one last time to submit, otherwise our artillery will know how to impose our will upon you."

The *panglima* cried out in rage:

"Ah! So that is how it is going to be! Well! At least we shall be avenged!"

And he ran towards the Sakay to give the order to execute the prisoners. But, at that very moment, as though the result of the setting in motion of some great clockwork, an awful whining was heard in the air, and a shell came crashing down on one of the straw huts in the Toko, strewing about its debris. Men fell, curses burst out. A second bomb left its trail through the sky and, this time, fell amongst the Sakay—it was a massacre.

Wilhelm had told the truth. At the precise moment the bombardment began, the Dutch troops broke through the gates of the *kraton*.

The artillery raged on. The Aceh and Sakay were fleeing from the missiles raining down upon them. The officer grabbed a weapon and, leading his wife and children, he sought to cut his way through the crowd.

But would Wilhelm and his family not be hit? The Aceh's panic, at least, gave them some hope of escape.

"Listen!" said Wilhelm to Luisa, "I can hear our soldiers' bugles. They've forced open the doors; they'll be here in a few minutes. Have courage! Hold Margaret tightly to your chest. George, don't leave me!"

And he continued to advance under the hail of steel and fire which miraculously spared him. Already, the Dutch uniforms were appearing on the walls of Kota-Rajia; the artillery, well directed, modified its firing to give the attackers an open field.

"We're saved!" cried out Wilhelm.

But, at this very moment, Igli-Otou, who did not wish to see his victims escape, and who had followed their trail, seized upon a moment when little George, in spite of all his efforts, had lagged back a few steps. He sprang on the child, snatched him away, ran off between the huts, losing himself in the ruins, and disappeared.

He held the child tightly. The sorcerer believed in his magic. By autosuggestion, he was convinced that his God, Antou, a shapeless idol he served in the forests of

Malacca, required a human sacrifice. If the blood of a white man was shed, offered to that monstrous divinity, all these cataclysms, the bombardment, the screeching of the shells, the march of the enemy troops clambering up the ramparts, all would suddenly stop—and the Dutch would be struck down.

He had taken little George, and, leaping amongst the rocks which overhung the *kraton*, managed to finally reach a platform which sloped sharply over a fissure so dark and so deep as to appear bottomless. It was a favorable spot. He dropped the child heavily upon the cold stone, then raising his eyes towards the sky in an invocation, he drew a dagger from his belt, the blade of which was notched like the jaw of a crocodile.

George saw this, was horrified, and wanted to cry out, but the hand of Igli-Otou nailed him to the ground, while the other raised the horrible weapon.

Suddenly, a form which seemingly appeared out of nowhere, dropped in a gigantic leap from a stone above and landed heavily on the platform. It grabbed Igli-Otou by the scruff of the neck, raised him in the air like a puppet, then, with a sudden release, dropped him down the fissure. The Sakay smacked against the wall, spread out his arms, scratched the granite with his nails, whirled and disappeared.

The child had remained in place, motionless, having fainted away. The ape-man, the mysterious creature, then knelt, took the child in his arms, approached his lips as though to kiss him, and, supporting him against his chest, allowed himself to quickly drop to the bottom of the rock, ran, reached some woods, plunged into them, and disappeared, taking George with him.

The hand of Igli-Otou nailed him to the ground

Chapter VI

For hours on end, the escapee from Rota-Rajia ran out, with his prey, his conquest, after the Sun set, in the deepest night, without hesitation, without a break.

In astonishing dashes, crossing a chasm, climbing a rock, leaping over a pit, he went, holding the fainted and motionless child tight against his chest. This frail human frame had been subjected to such jolts, both in mind and body, that its brain had plunged into a coma. However, it seemed that the great creature understood this weakness. With an incredible dexterity, it drew aside all that could have struck and hurt the infant he carried, and, when he hung suspended by one arm from the branch of a tree, when he dropped from high up onto his feet, he did so in such a manner that the child was not subject to any violent shocks.

At first, he had charged through the undergrowth, following a straight-ahead path through the tangled jungle, with a strength of will resolved to attain its goal; nothing, however, in his behavior suggested any calculation. He was guided by instinct alone, by one of those natural faculties one may find among carrier pigeons. He dashed forward so forcefully, his rush so irresistible, that the way opened before him. As soon as he had passed, the branches dropped again, closed up, recreating an impenetrable barrier behind him.

Sometimes, when a tree stood before him, a *foualang* with hard, unbreakable branches, whose colossal trunk six men holding hands could not have spanned, the fugitive, pausing for a moment, flexed his legs, and, in a prodigious muscular release, shot like a stone from a sling, reached another branch, let himself hang so as to catch one further on, and thus, by way of a trapeze exercise, before which the most agile of our clowns would have backed away, he arrived at a small clearing. There, he allowed himself to drop to the ground and resume his dizzying race.

Thus, he traveled further and further on, into solitudes where man had never penetrated, into masses of greenery, foliage, of great seedlings as deep as waves upon the sea, through a colonnade of trees so tightly packed, so thick-set that sometimes he had trouble slipping through. Then, he would break the younger stems and still make his way through.

Sometimes, it was the tree-ferns which surrounded him, tried to tie him up, grabbing him by the neck, the legs, the arms. He fought, braced himself, but always made it through, under the rains from the dew on the canopy, tramping through the sticky mud which he hammered with his feet to find some release.

Water accumulated by the moisture of the vegetation, which remained in milky greenish ponds, gushing springs spurting from some fault in the rock, struck him as he passed, causing such a violent shock as to draw a *heh!* of defiance, a pause to draw breath—had the child been struck? No, he had bent over in time and with his flesh and fur had protected him.

To the treacherous forest had succeeded the mountain, more brutal with its precipitous slopes, its exposed knolls, its black diamond spires, its piles of crumbled rocks strewn here and there by some internal upheavals, with, all of a sudden, a dug-out bowl, the crater of an extinct volcano, whose clean and slippery sides offered no grip for walking. His feet adapted themselves and the flight continued.

For 30 hours, the mysterious creature had thus fought against Nature. Night had passed, then a day, then another night. The Sun rose, irradiating the immensity of the landscape with its vivid and splendid glow. They were now in a small, upland valley, halfway up the mountain, in a clearing girt with giant trees, which encompassed a gorge lined with mosses and small bushes.

The man-ape slowed his pace, stopped, looked around, picked out a clump of trees forming a sort of canopy. Then, in the white light, he gazed upon the child with an odd grin, quickly prepared a pile of leaves, and then put his burden down upon it.

The poor little George was pale, as if exsanguinated. Why did he not move? the creature wondered. Very soft sounds escaped from his throat, made up of vowels combined with strong consonants, recalling the Spanish *jota* or the German *ch*, odd contractions of the glottis which nonetheless had a certain sonority of melancholy and worry. He knelt down and his huge mouth almost touched that of the little boy, as if to draw in his breath.

The man-ape got up suddenly. He had felt a breath caress his face. The child was alive! But why this immobility? Why this silence? Why did these frail limbs he held up drop back inert, as if paralyzed? He drew back slightly, his head falling to his chest, his eyes wide open in a mask of mental strain and thought. Certainly, a question remained, still unfathomable, as the frowning of his eyebrows and the pouting of his lips attested.

But, all of a sudden, his lips relaxed. He raised his head, and his mobile features brightened. He had figured it out! A personal sensation, that of hunger, had brought on a simple deduction. The child, too, must be hungry, and it was with this condition that one could associate his depressed state. He uttered several times a single syllable:

"*Ete! Ete!*"

He raised his head and saw, some distance away, some lianas that were well known to him and which the natives called *Akar-Loodany*. They contained a lovely and nourishing liquid, while their seeds, milky and wholesome, make an excellent food. However, he was separated from this green clump by a deep gulf, a split right through the bedrock, which had accumulated the prevailing humidity in a muddy cesspool. It was a matter of getting across it.

Again, the man-ape came up with a solution: two enormous branches were arranged, one before the other, not forming a bridge, but as bars which could serve as an aerial route. He took a step forward, ready to take a running start, yet he stopped, and came back. He hesitated to move away from the child, knowing that these solitudes hid terrible treacheries, slimy creatures slithering beneath the tree limbs, wild beasts lurking in the brush.

All was calm; there was not a sound, not a murmur. The child was well, quietly laying on the bed of moss, the tree branches above his head forming a protective cradle. In this deep repose, his breathing was regular, even some color was apparent on his cheeks. Everything was reassuring. The creature made a gesture of decision and, at a resolute pace, ran to the chasm, still turning his head towards the motionless child. He took a running start, jumped, reached the first branch the extremity of which bent under his weight, but not sufficiently that he could not manage to grab onto the other, stronger branch. Thus, in an alternating motion, throwing out his arms one after the other, he managed to reach the other side of the dark gulf, slid down, tore off handfuls of the nutritious liana, which he hung from his neck and shoulders, and, with little squeals of joy, took up once more his perilous way, suspended from the branch which had already held him up.

But, suddenly there was a cracking sound... The branch broke and he was thrown and dropped onto the slippery slope of the chasm. Were he to fall down to the bottom, it would mean a certain and most agonizing death, as the deep, viscous mud would snatch him up, envelop him, and suck him in. He knew this, and where his fingers were sunk in like steel pins, he held on desperately with his nails.

But the material was not hard enough; he felt it crumble and slip through his fingers. He stuck his heels into the saturated soil, and still he had that horrible sensation that it was all giving way under his weight. At the same time, a horrible cry rang out, terrifying high pitched—the voice of the child, who. from his tight throat, was calling for help!

What was happening? The torpor in which George had sunk, long maintained by the brutality of the journey and the continuous shaking movement, dissipated little by little. The fresh air, which came down from the canopy, penetrated his limbs and released them of their stiffness. It was almost a feeling of well-being, mixed, however, with a little fever-driven excitation, which did not allow him to fully clear his thoughts. He opened his eyes, and by the radiant glow of the dawn, filtered through the trees, saw the strange and magnificent spectacle of the vast forest, with its colossal trees, its inextricably tangled boughs, their vault taller than those of the largest cathedrals.

He thought he was dreaming and closed his eyes, only to open them again. And it was then that he let out a desperate cry, drawn from all the terrors of his night-mare. A monstrous ape had just leaped out from the depths of the underbrush, a true ape, a Maoussa, an orangutan, huge, deformed, its belly distended, its limbs knotted, its legs short and bending under the weight of its colossal torso. Its face was grimacing. Near the horri-ble snubnose, the eyes, stupid and malevolent, blinked.

From the height of his aerial observation point, the ape had seen the child stretched out, and born in him was a nasty, bestial instinct to acquire this unknown prey, for he had never seen anything like it, as no human being had yet penetrated the mysterious depths of Sumatra's innermost forests.

Was it a carnivore's appetite which drew him? No, since even of the fiercest of apes don't feed upon flesh. He obeyed a brute instinct, a desire to destroy. Dropping from branch to branch, he hastened towards the child. Were poor George to end up between its huge paws, strangulation, dismemberment, and the breaking of his bones on the rocks, would likely be the result of the un-restrained beast's furious and disgusting game.

Had George guessed all of this? He had only seen the animal when it was about to land on the ground, and in his child's imagination, the vision proved fantastic, demonic. He had cried out with all his strength, with all his breath, without knowing or understanding where he was, without even having the notion that he could be rescued. And one word had burst forth from his mouth, that word which all little children utter and which, some-times, returns to the lips of the elderly in their last mo-ments:

"Mommy! Mommy!"

The cry had been so high-pitched that the ape had paused for an instant. The brute, being cowardly, was prudent. From up there, he had thought he could attack with impunity a creature which would not even try to defend itself. He knew all the denizens of the forests and mountains; he knew which he was sure to subdue, and those before which he must flee.

He was almost scared of this little fellow who had suddenly risen to his feet and, petrified with surprise, horrified, was watching him wild-eyed. He got on all fours, hiking up his back, circling around the child, stopping to scratch himself, then again taking a few steps back and then forward.

"Mommy! Mommy!" repeated desperately little George.

The ape soon convinced himself that this stranger was very weak, at his mercy; he leaped on him in one last bound. Feeling the ape's claws on his body, George, startled, drew back and tried to escape. But, more alert, the monster caught up with him. His nails penetrated the boy's clothing. The fabric tore, stayed attached to the ape's claws, who furiously shook his hand. Then, having decided to get it over with, he resolutely threw himself upon the child, who, this time, was caught. The beast began to drag him by his arms towards the forest, grinding its teeth in rage. George was struggling, screaming, trying to tear his wrists from the hold.

The ape, exasperated, rising on his legs, threw hands around the child's neck.

"Mommy! Mommy!" screamed the child.

Suddenly, the ape received a violent blow right in the forehead, which made him roll to the ground. The savior had come. The mysterious creature who, seeing the child at risk at exactly the instant he felt himself slipping into the abyss, had made a supreme, desperate attempt to escape, and had managed to leap onto the crest of the gulf. And now, he was before the child, raising his huge bulk, his great hands darting out against the assailant.

Suddenly the ape received a violent blow right in the forehead, which made him roll on the ground.

The latter, having gotten himself up, did not run away. His simian face was twitching and his blinking eyes showed flashes of rage, while from his throat came high-pitched, inarticulate, bugle-like cries. Relaxing his hamstrings, he charged his adversary, recognizing in him his primordial enemy, he who, issued of the same lineage, despised and abhorred him. Once again, he let out his guttural cry.

Between the two creatures, one the ape, the other the half-man, the battle was engaged, furious, to the death. The ape was tremendously strong; the man-ape, the colossus, was no less powerful, but what distinguished him from the brute was the coordination of his movements and the attention he brought to defending himself. While the ape, time and time again, struck out wildly with his limbs, in instinctive, disordered motions, the other, more master of himself, struck out straight ahead and with accuracy.

The muffled blows rang out frightfully; they finally clinched, the ape seizing his adversary with all four hands, wrapping him up with his arms and legs. In this bestial charge, the ape left himself open; the other's hands closed around his throat, tightening, choking, and as the ape rattled out his last beath, the victor carried him towards the muddy abyss, into which he pitched him.

The ape gave out one last screech, an awful agonizing outcry, then disappeared. But upon this last cry, which might have been a call, apes of all sizes appeared upon the tree limbs, rushing to the aid of their comrade. The man-ape, his task accomplished, had come back towards George in the nick of time, just as the group of apes approached. He perceived the awful danger: this crowd of apes would surround the two of them. It was a horrible, unequal battle.

Quickly, he seized the child and placed him behind him, against a rock, against which, with an elementary sense of strategy, he backed up, sheltering the child with his body. Then, finding within his grasp a young tree trunk, he tore it out with one twist and thus, he drew himself up, like a great athlete, ready to receive the attack. It was not long in coming. The apes were the first to charge him, throwing out their arms before them as though seeking to harpoon him, while others, tumbling down from the trees, armed themselves with missiles, fruits, broken branches, with which they bombarded him.

The man-ape struck, breaking limbs, cracking open skulls, but the apes were not getting discouraged; their instinct told them that they would eventually manage to tire him out, more so since the little one, terror-struck, held on desperately to his rescuer's legs, and was in danger of paralyzing him.

Already a number of missiles had struck the fighter, who now had bloody traces on his brown face. The terrible windmill of his arm was slowing; it was only moments before he would weaken. Then, in turn, he let out an oddly modulated cry, which surely could not simply be the cry of a beast, having two very clear syllables:

"*To-Ho! To-Ho!*"

And then, in the distance, other calls answered him:

"*To-Ho! To-Ho!*"

The apes, completely wrapped up in their bestial exasperation, had neither heard, nor understood the meaning of the cry. Perhaps they thought it was a desperate cry of agony. The man-ape, however, was bolstered by a new hope, as he felt himself overwhelmed by the enemy's numbers. He tried to expend an ultimate effort. Gathering all his strength, he took hold of a large fragment of rock, which he had managed to shake loose, and, having pulled it out, rolled it in front of him and stuck it in the ground as a barricade.

Under this provisional cover, which at least subtracted a portion of his body from the apes' strikes, he fought on, lashing out at the overly audacious amongst his assailants. But, on their side, the apes had numbers, stubbornness, and an instinct for evil. They tried to surprise him, climbing up the tree trunks, jumping from there onto the rock which covered his back, dangling from lianas and trying to tear him apart with their nails. Another instant and the whole horde was going to drop on his shoulders, crush him under their weight. His strength was giving out.

"*To-Ho! To-Ho!*"

All of a sudden, there was a tremendous stampede coming through the forest, a frantic push bursting through the brush and undergrowth:

"*To-Ho! To-Ho!*"

A group of huge creatures, seemingly both human and simian at once, brandishing sticks or holding sharp stones in their hands, threw themselves upon the apes.

It was a stunning and grotesque scene of horror! The apes were taken with an indescribable panic. On their distorted masks, terror stretched their muscles in convulsive contractions, and it was a leaping, tumbling, stunning *mêlée* to escape. Hideous and ridiculous, they pushed each other, threw each other over, in an excruciating cacophony of yelps. Those arriving chased them down, bludgeoning those they could reach, slashing the others with their stones.

Amongst them there were some females, of great size: one of them, coming out through the ranks, rushed towards the injured creature. With one muscular exertion, she threw over the stone behind which he had sheltered himself and took him in her arms, hugging him, seeking to staunch the blood that flowed over his face and coagulated on his hairy torso. She whispered softly the two syllables: "*To-Ho! To-Ho!*" It was clearly his own name, which he had called out through the forest as a signal; it was the same his mate repeated as she lavished signs of affection upon him.

But, suddenly, she saw the child, who, terrified, still thinking himself in a nightmare, hung desperately onto the one he knew to be his friend and defender. The female, in an instinctive and terrified gesture, wished to push him away. The little one began to moan. To-Ho heard, and, spreading his big lips in a smile of goodwill, he spoke a few syllables to his mate. She shrugged her shoulders, with a sort of tremor of disbelief and revolt. But To-Ho placed his large hand on the child's head, saying something again, in a plaintive tone, in which tears were held back, and the female suddenly had a down-cast look, big tears even beading under her eyelids.

She then took the child in her arms and looked at him for a long time. She made a gesture of decision, put the child on one of her shoulders and held out her arm to To-Ho. He leaned on it.

The others, males and females, seemed to be prey to a profound happiness, undoubtedly for having arrived in time and having dispersed the apes, their eternal enemies. The younger ones gave themselves up to wild dances, stepping to a rhythm they accompanied with strange cries resembling a barbarian chant. And, upon a new cry from To-Ho, they all gathered around him and his mate who carried the child. George had thrown his two arms around her neck and was falling asleep, exhausted.

The tribe plunged into the forest.

Part Two: Margaret's Dream

Chapter I

What had happened in Kota-Rajia?

The Dutch assault, supported by their well-aimed artillery, had overcome the Aceh's desperate resistance; throughout the smoking ruins, the victors had pursued, tracked down and massacred the *kraton*'s defenders, despite their heroic struggle. The *panglima* of 22 *moukims* held in check the attackers at the Three-Tiered Mountain; the Sakay had regrouped themselves around him and, to the last, fought to the death.

The Sultan, nestled in his palace, as the fatalistic Muslim that he was, waited for Allah's decision, for a conclusion to the events. All the bearers of bad tidings had been massacred before his eyes, by his order. By not knowing the truth, he could ignore it. At last, the ramparts had collapsed, and Colonel van der Hyeden had forced his way over a bridge of piled up corpses of the Sultan's making, into the mausoleum whose doors were broken open. Mahmoud Shah, apparently impassive, waited for him, crouching on his throne, showing no sign of fear.

But the victors intended to spare his life. They knew well that his submission would not be long delayed, given his cowardice and financial needs. Thus was it arranged.

The pirates' last stronghold was destroyed, and the Dutchmen's hurrahs saluted their triumph. Then, after some quick negotiations with the Sultan's councilors, van der Hyeden summoned all his officers, and, in a solemn gesture, planted the Dutch flag on the ramparts of the defeated fortress.

Then, looking around him, he said:

"I do not see Captain Villiers. However, I was assured that he had not perished in this dreadful adventure; he was in mourning, I wish him to be honored."

"Here he is! Here he is!" voices cried out, while the ranks opened up.

Captain Villiers had indeed just appeared, but so pale, bearing on his countenance the traces of such profound despair that the Colonel, who had quickly moved forward to meet him, stopped, aghast.

"What has happened then?" he cried out. "I had been told that, during the heroic mission that you so valiantly fulfilled, you had the unbelievable good fortune of rejoining, right here, your wife and children."

"My children," the Captain said sadly, shaking his head. "Ah! How truly you speak, Colonel! Yes, at the very moment the Aceh Sultan sent me off to die, I had the ineffable joy of marching to execution with my dear wife, she who the executioners called Mayha, and with us were our two children, George, so handsome, so valiant, and Margaret, my dearest little girl. And truly, having so long been separated in life, it seemed a comfort that we would all be reunited in death! But alas, fate was not yet defeated!"

"What do you mean?"

"That in the middle of the bombardment, as I was making my way with my own son, my poor George disappeared, and all my efforts to find him again have remained useless."

The unhappy father burst into sobs.

"But perhaps not all hope is lost?" replied the Colonel, moved to sadness. "Perhaps the child got lost, perhaps he was injured? I will order a search to be made."

"Alas! Colonel, all this has been tried: the poor mother has had the sad courage of looking at the injured and the dead one by one. Our child was not among them. No sign of where he has gone has been discovered, and it may be that this ignorance of his fate is even more upsetting than the certitude of a catastrophe!"

What could one answer? What consolation could one offer to a father so cruelly stricken?

All of Captain Villiers' comrades in arms put themselves at his disposal and conscientiously employed themselves in trying to unravel this sinister mystery.

Finally, a Sakay prisoner spoke, with a dark happiness, savoring the suffering he brought to his enemy. He stated that the child had been kidnapped by Igli-Otou. He had seen him, he swore by the great Antou, and as he indicated the direction taken by the Sakay sorcerer, a search was begun throughout the surrounding area.

If one had to, one would pursue the miserable kidnapper to the depths of the Malay peninsula, one would search the country, one would sack it until these savages would hand back their prisoner. Captain Villiers would take command of the expedition and the criminal's punishment would be awful! But one had to give up on this last hope as the mutilated, yet still recognizable, corpse of Igli-Otou lay at the bottom of the abyss. How had he been hurled there? An awful detail: he still held, in his clenched hand, the belt which had been at the child's waist!

The still recognizable corpse of Igli-Otou lay at the bottom of the abyss.

Therefore, no doubt remained. While it was true that one never found poor George's body, beneath the place where the broken body of Igli-Otou had come to rest, a torrent passed, losing itself in the depths of the mountain. The child's body must have been carried away, and even if he had miraculously survived this horrible death, he would have gotten lost in the jungle, and become prey to the wild beasts.

No doubt could remain. The father's despair was frightening, yet less than the state of prostration into which the wretched Louisa had fallen. It seemed that all the springs of life had suddenly snapped within her. Villiers long feared that she would lose her mind. They had

had to separate her from little Margaret, whom she no longer seemed to recognize, and repeated fits of hysterics left it in question whether she would live.

A few months passed in this manner. The conquest was being consolidated. Colonel van der Hyeden, in the hope of softening the Captain's sadness, promoted him to a higher rank, then offered him one of the most important posts in the new colony. While there was a time when Villiers and his wife had had a passionate attachment to this wonderful country, where Nature is awe-inspiring, where the Sun lavishes life and beauty to all, now, staying on the island had become insufferable. Luisa's health, far from improving, seemed forever compromised. Wounded to the depths of her heart, she was haunted by fantastic visions. Madness lay in wait for her. Villiers had to resolve the situation in a decisive manner.

He went to his superior, and explained the difficult circumstances with which he wrestled. Clearly, it was a great tragedy for him to break his sword, but destiny had decided his fate. He resigned his commission and announced his departure for Europe. Besides, he seemed to have aged ten years; it was clear that he could no longer sustain the rigors of colonial service.

The Colonel, now General van der Hyeden, not only did not oppose his resolution, but testified of his respect and friendship for him. With profound regret did he view his separation from this devoted serviceman, this steadfast and generous friend, but why fight the inevitable? He could not but yield to his request.

Villiers shipped out to Europe with his wife and daughter, and returned to Rotterdam, the city of his birth. There it was that they had loved each other, married, and where their children had been born. Might they not rediscover there some peace and quiet, and, if not the forgetfulness, then the abatement of their sorrows? They retired to their old family home in Hoogstraat, a few paces from the Groote Market. It was one of those old mansions which mysteriously preserve under its black stones the sadness of many generations.

He resigned his commission and announced his departure for Europe.

For a long time, Luisa's health had been shaky; the shock to her system was only slowly fading. The least incident that woke her terrible memories plunged her back into dangerous hysterics. Villiers had tried to tear himself away from his worries by devoting himself to starting a business. His brother, Peter Villiers, a chemist, who had, when the catastrophe took place, planned to join them in Sumatra, had done all his power in order to stimulate new interests in him.

As director of the famed Vanderheim Co., which owned gold mines and held investments throughout the world, he had made William an associate in the business. But the latter, while conscientiously fulfilling the administrative functions he had accepted, was entirely indifferent to the ambitious schemes his brother revealed to him.

The years passed and time, which softens the greatest sorrows exerted its beneficent influence on Wilhelm and his wife. But as healed as she was, the wound they received was still painful.

What of Margaret? She had grown up and was now 16. She was a beautiful tall young lady, graced with blond hair and blue eyes, the admirable complexion of Dutch girls, and the fine constitution she held from her French heritage. She was devoted to her mother with all the passion of a loving daughter. She remembered the terrible events she had been mixed up in her childhood, and had not forgotten her dear little brother, who had been so good to her and whom she had already considered as her protector. She had taken on the mission of doubly cherishing her mother, for her sake, and for that of the one she had lost.

Luisa enumerated to herself these tokens of great goodwill and was most beholden to her, but she could not forget her son, who would now be almost 20, and on whose arm she would have leaned. How proud she would have been to see him, tall and handsome, strolling on the great Rosenboom promenade! And in the smiles she gave her daughter, there always remained a crease of eternal regret, with the thought—that is the selfishness of mothers—that the day would come when a man would take her daughter far away, leaving her alone with her anguish.

Her only joy, most precarious indeed, was to read all that was recently published regarding the island of Sumatra. Was it an unavowed hope that guided her? Did she hope, one day, to find a clue, a detail overlooked by all that would reveal the existence of her son? She no longer believed, no longer wanted to acknowledge his death, and, oddly enough, when, slightly feverish, she stated to Margaret that her brother was still alive, that she felt him, that she sensed him, the young girl did not refute her, but shook her head and whispered:

"Why not?"

One day, in the *Rotterdamsche Dagblad*, Luisa Villiers came across an article. A lecture was being given at the Academy of Sciences titled: EXPLORATIONS IN CENTRAL SUMATRA: GOLD MINES. MAN'S ANCESTOR. Margaret had noticed this announcement, but had not pointed it out to her mother, out of fear that, in reading the name of the lecturer, she might give away her ingenuous awkwardness by the trembling of her voice. For not too long ago, a young doctor with ties to the Vanderheim Co. had said to Margaret:

"Will you be my bride?"

Margaret had blushed, but her eyes had not said no.

"Your bride?" she spoke softly. "I'm rather young and perhaps we shall have to wait quite some time. Besides, you know of the bereavement that hangs over my parents' home. You know the sad state of my mother... I neither want to, nor could ever leave her. My only role here on Earth is to replace the son she lost."

"I know of this terrible adventure," had replied Frederik Leven—such was the young man's name. "But, in turn, listen to me. Do you yourself believe in your brother's death?"

"Alas, how can one have any doubt of it? Still...."

"Tell me honestly what you are thinking. I am and always will be your friend. You can trust me."

"Well, then... Please don't laugh at me... I have a sort of persistent, unshakeable feeling that tells me that my brother is still alive... Do you believe in dreams?"

"Hmm," answered the scientist, smiling. "I have little faith in the incredible. Nonetheless, who knows? As Hamlet said 'there are greater mysteries between Heaven and Earth than are dreamt of in your philosophy.' Speak with no fear of being ridiculed."

"Well, here it is… At night, in a sort of half-waking state, I see my brother again... Not as child, but as a man, big and strong, as I knew my father... He is surrounded by strange creatures that resemble apes, but aren't really, as they speak... He leads the life of a savage, but with some semblance of a primitive civilization. I well know that what I tell you must seem crazy... Yet, the power of this vision, the constant repetition of the same details, has led me to this belief... I have never spoken of it to my poor mother, though… A thousand times, I wished to tell her of my thoughts. If my dreams were true! If my brother still lived in the depths of the central island, in those forests where, I have been told, no European has ever penetrated…"

Frederik had not interrupted the young girl.

"I do not believe in dreams," he said at last. "I believe in science... But, oddly enough, the slumber-borne illusions you have described to me concur with certain, yet unconfirmed but plausible reports. A number of explorers have stated that, in Java and in Sumatra, there exists, or has existed, creatures which would occupy a position midway between the simian and human races. This is a most fascinating problem, and it is my intention to attempt to solve it."

"What do you mean?"

"This—if I was so forward as to ask for your hand in marriage… If, having until now hidden the deepest emotions you evoke in me, I asked you whether you would be betrothed to my heart, it is because I am planning to leave Holland."

"To leave Holland!"

"Yes. I have been hired by the Vanderheim Co. to lead an exploration in the island of Sumatra, where, according to all accounts, large gold deposits are to be found. I will be gone for at least two years and I wished to bring along with me some hope that you would consent to become my companion in years to come. Will you give me such hope?"

"With all my heart, but remember that I will never leave my mother."

"I remember, but who knows what the future will bring. I promise that I will, at the very least, make every possible attempt to rediscover, if it is possible after so many years, traces of your brother. What if your dream were to be true after all?"

Then, Frederik Leven had left.

Margaret had followed, step by step, in the Javanese newspapers, the news of the explorer, who had faced many dangers and, little by little, developed a well-deserved reputation of courage and erudition. He was now on his way back, and the announcement of his conference was like a calling card that fell under the immediate scrutiny of she who had stayed his betrothed in both heart and soul.

Mrs. Villiers did not know any of this. Young women have their little secrets which they like to keep in the deepest recesses of their soul. And did Margaret not know that she had not the right to leave her mother? What good could come from inflicting a new sorrow upon her? However, Mrs. Villiers seemed particularly interested by the announcement.

"Frederik Leven!" she exclaimed in reading the newspaper. "Was he not the young man in which your father was so interested, and whom we have on several occasions met in the past?"

"Yes, indeed, I believe so," said the young woman.

"I know that Wilhelm thought highly of him. He often told me that, had our poor George lived, he would have liked him to be like this young man. Listen, Margaret," added Louisa, with an unusual restlessness, "if you wish, we shall attend his lecture."

"Dearest mother!" the young girl cried out as she ran to Luisa and wrapped her arms around her neck. Mrs. Villiers did not guess the emotion which provoked this demonstration of affection.

"So you'll come along with me?"

"With great pleasure"

"Fine! We'll discuss it with your father tonight."

Villiers did not have, as one would expect, any objections to put forth. As for himself, he would forego it, since he never went out at night, nor sought any distractions outside business hours. However, he declared that he found Frederik Leven a most likable fellow, and that Mr. Vanderheim held him in great esteem, especially since his investigations had apparently been crowned with success, and that he had brought back some of the most complete information on the gold mines and primitive races of Sumatra.

Margaret listened, attentive and pleasurably troubled. Thus she spent the few days before the arrival of the steamer bearing Frederik Leven in a heightened emotional state. With what great joy she went, on that special day, to sit with her mother, in the front row of the great hall of the Academy of Sciences, which occupies, as is well known, a palace near the Stock Exchange on the Blaak pier.

A royal magistrate attended the meeting, and all of the city's officials were there as well, wishing to show their esteem towards the young explorer. Eight o'clock rang. A great hush fell on the crowd.

Frederik Leven appeared at the podium. Blond, with thick hair pulled up on a wide and bulging brow, handsome in his high-buttoned frock-coat, in a near military stance, he discreetly acknowledged the assembly who welcomed him with a salvo of applause. However, in his first survey of the crowd, he had picked out she towards whom, during his long absence, all his thoughts had been turned. Amid the crowd that knew nothing of this idyll, two gazes met, renewing the past's delicate chain and a promise of the future.

In a very short speech, the burgmeister of Rotterdam introduced the young speaker, a child of the ancient city of the Four Lions,[15] who well deserved the praise of former colonists for his services, and who, all hoped, would renew and expand commerce. He then gave the floor to Frederik Leven.

Without emphasis, with a simplicity not without charm, the young man began his presentation. He spoke of the superb vistas of the island he had explored; he described the progress achieved since the conquest, the

---

[15] These emblems appear on the city's coat of arms.

happy condition of the islanders, and the blessing of a fair and almost paternal administration. The insurrections were increasingly rare. The European rule, capable in its handling of the country's sensitive issues, was accepted in good faith.

Chapter II

The naturally somewhat optimistic picture which the affable and high-toned speaker outlined was met with signs of unanimous approval. This allowed the young man to address, in a more than simply rhetorical manner, the obligation of the conquerors to bring civilization to the natives.

"All violence," he said, "breeds violence. Our role is to persuade, to teach, to raise the thoughts and conscience. In this only is the justification for conquest."

Margaret thanked the speaker with a slight bow of her head. Encouraged, he moved on to the second item of his presentation: information gathered on the country's mineral riches.

They were considerable, but difficult to exploit. One needed to proceed methodically, first to clear the land, then to build roads. Turning to a blackboard, he indicated with a few chalk lines the island's system of waterways, showing in which directions the penetration should occur. In addition, one must especially not forget that the wilds were infested with fierce beasts, who, for centuries, had made them their domain.

He had documented the existence of precious minerals, and had brought back the proof that a well-organized exploration would reap great rewards; however—and here, he drew his listeners' complete attention to one of the strangest facts he had been given to witness—long hence had the island been visited by prospectors, who had boldly, at the risk of their very lives, penetrated inland to the unexplored regions.

On a number of occasions, they had thought the goal of their ambitions in hand, only to have their hopes dashed by an as yet unexplained phenomenon.

It is well known that gold is rarely found as pure nuggets, or even as easily recognizable and collectable specks. In general, their discovery serves as an indication of where to search for larger deposits of pyrites, gold-bearing quartz, of sulphurous ores that make up what is termed the main lode. Guided by the discovery of small quantities of free gold, the prospectors ventured to the most inaccessible locations of the central plateau, frequently identifying what were clearly large deposits.

Encouraged by their findings, they returned to the population centers, bearing a few ounces of gold powder gathered on their way to prove the truth of their tales. An expedition was organized and pushed into the mountainous solitudes, to the region of Merapi... and here was where the mystery began.

On their way, the explorers found only very rare traces of gold, infinitesimal and worthless. When they reached the deposits of pyrites or quartz that had excited their lust— justified by the analysis that had been made of the material— all they found before them were black muddy masses wherein not a trace of gold could be found!

"I myself followed one of these expeditions," said the speaker, "and every time, the prospectors statements were refuted by the actual discoveries."

The prosperctors defended their good faith with an energy which was certainly not without some probative value. Was one to believe that, in their passion for the discovery of gold, they had been the victims of some kind of mirage? The young speaker would not venture to say, but he was certain that, without pushing all the way into the unknown regions, it was possible, even easy, to carry on mining operations that would return handsome dividends on the funds invested.

His experience as a geologist had definitely assured him of the presence of gold-bearing minerals, and the diagrams and mineral samples he had brought back would convince even the most incredulous investor. If expeditions were undertaken methodically, and not in the excited state under which ignorant prospectors operated, wandering off at random, not following any scientific mode of inquiry, they could be successful. Following his speech he would present the minerals he had personally gathered and which would support his assertions.

However, before ending his talk, there remained a most singular and important question to deal with, as it concerned the history of humankind, its origin and its development.

"First of all," continued the speaker, "I must tell you of the explanation given by the natives for the prospectors' lack of success. According to them, these prospectors did indeed find gold, did indeed discover deposits, and even the Acehs and Battaks assert that there are caves entirely carpeted in gold, with the precious metal rising from the rock in needles—although that description is likely the product of their inflamed imagination. But they claim that these treasures are guarded by monstrous creatures which devote themselves to keeping it from men, their enemies. If a human manages to discover the caves' existence, they destroy him. These mysterious creatures are called the *Tang-Tomis* in Malay, the Gold Destroyers!

"Naturally, you will understand," continued Leven, "the disbelief with which I greeted such yarns. However, when I studied these tales, which differ in their details, I found certain common threads. I've become convinced that, on the high plateaus, isolated from the rest of the world by impenetrable thickets, there exist what are probably very small tribes, which, however, bear most interesting characteristics. Let me state my thoughts in all candor: these tribes are comprised of creatures who may constitute what Darwin termed the "missing link," a being intermediate between our simian ancestors and man!"

Here the speaker was suddenly interrupted:

"It is not true that man is descended from apes! Darwin is a fraud."

Very calmly, almost smiling, Leven allowed the storm to pass, supported by the near unanimous applause of his listeners. Finally, raising his hand, he begged for silence, his presence overcoming the trouble-makers.

"My colleagues," he said, "I make allowances for all points of view, and would be most saddened were I to offend anyone, but I am before all a man of science and stick to established facts. I maintain that there exists in Sumatra—or at least existed at one time—beings which, while not exactly like men, were however entirely superior to apes. This is what I propose to show you. My assertions are supported by the discovery of skeletal remains I made myself in Sumatra. I see amongst those assembled here the venerable master-scientist Valtenius, the world's premier anatomist, to whom scientists of all countries pay homage. I beg him to come forward and examine the skeletal remains of which I speak, and give his opinion."

Dr. Valtenius, a true glory of Dutch science, had rather retrograde opinions. He did not accept new ideas until they had passed through the crucible of the most exacting criticism, and did not accept Darwin and

Haeckel's theories without some serious restrictions. To appeal to his enlightenment was to prove one's impartiality and sincere desire to know the truth.

Valtenius—an elderly man with long white hair—rose and said aloud:

"Young man, I am at this assembly's disposal, but promise me not to bear a grudge if I destroy your illusions."

"Doctor, I give you my word to accept your opinion without uttering a single protest."

"Bravo! Bravo! Valtenius to the podium," said the crowd.

Upon a sign from Leven, assistants brought out a chest which they placed on the table. Valtenius, still nimble for his age, quickly climbed the stage steps, impatient to examine the remains which were being presented him. Everyone rose in their seats to see better. Leven looked at Margaret and noticed a shadow of concern on her face; no doubt, she was apprehensive that her friend might become the victim of public humiliation. With a small gesture of his hand, which only she could notice, he reassured her.

The chest was opened and the skeletal remains removed and spread out on the table. Leven stepped back to allow Dr. Valtenius every liberty in making his examination.

The Doctor's face had, during this initial preparation, borne an ironic smile, the meaning of which was clear to everyone: these young whippersnappers, how easily were they led into false hypotheses! How quickly this one would fall back from dreams to harsh reality! But now, silence returned, profound and respectful.

Valtenius glanced at the bones spread out before him, and let out an exclamation of surprise; he bent over, placed a pair of glasses on his nose, and took up each bone one by one, weighing them, trying to ferret out their secrets, as it were.

"It's incredible!" he finally admitted.

"Speak! Speak!" rose from every mouth.

A current of curiosity swept over the room. The demon of science held sway over everyone and tightened their chests.

"I need a chair," said Valtenius. "I don't know... The excitement... My legs are like putty under me..."

As the assistants rushed to obey him, he drew himself up, then violently pushed back the chair which tumbled down, and standing up, began to speak:

"This is unheard of! Preposterous!" he clamored. "These are not the bones of a man, nor those of an ape... And the skull..." He let his fingers travel over a portion of the cranium, which he spun like a top: "Roughly 600 cm^3 of brain, while no human brain occupies less than 1100 or 1200 cm^3 and no ape, gorilla or orangutan has any more than 350 to 400 cm^3... This, an ape skull, never! But a man's skull, neither! It's somewhere in the middle."

"An ape? It can't be! Here, clearly delineated on the internal face of the skull are the convolutions of the brain, and that of articulate speech, so ably determined by Broca! They are visible, evident... They don't exist among the apes! But it isn't the skull of a man either, since even the most inferior races don't have a low and retreating brow, this prominent frontal beetling..."

He continued, in greater and greater excitement, brandishing a huge femur: "This isn't from an ape—an ape walks on all fours—it is from an animal with an upright stance. The bone is, however, stronger than in a man and the creature to which it belonged must have been a good tree climber."

"But," he continued, in greater and greater excitement, brandishing a huge femur.

"This creature... This man... Truly I don't know what to call it... would have stood some 1.70 meters tall, and—my goodness!—this tooth... You hadn't shown me this tooth... And this piece of jaw-bone... That's no ape jaw... Nor is that a man's... I must say, my young friend, that you were indeed correct: this creature is exactly half-way between man and ape!"

Margaret, transported with enthusiasm, interjected, "the missing link!" in a soft voice.

"So much for that!" Valtenius cried out. "I'm 76 and I've been through a lot, but—Goodness—I wasn't expecting, at my age, to be dealt such a blow! Ah! Young man," he added, raising his hand towards Leven, "you can boast of having raised quite a stir in me!"

He broke off, as if struck by a sudden idea, and spoke up again:

"Had he been right, that poor Van Kock, whom we all scoffed at? He who, after a trip to Java, had claimed to have seen with his own eyes the *Anthropopithecus*!"

"So, Doctor," Leven went on, "you admit that there could have existed—that there may exist—such creatures midway between man and ape?"

"Certainly! Yes, I admit it! Unless I were blind or lying, and I am neither. But I am dumbfounded! Would you like to come and discuss the matter further with me tomorrow morning?"

"Certainly, Doctor! It would be a great honor for me, and a great joy."

"Marvelous! And now, to show those assembled here that I hold you as my scientific equal—I will not say my superior, as I am unfortunately too old—let me embrace you."

And the good doctor placed on each of Leven's cheeks a resounding kiss. Lengthy applause saluted this act of scientific mentoring. Now order broke down, as everyone tried climbing on the stage and jostling one another in an effort to have a closer look at the remains of the *Anthropopithecus*, the ape-man.

Margaret had taken her mother along with her. She drew near Leven and, in a spontaneous gesture, extended her hand to him:

"Ah! You have no idea how happy I am!" she said softly.

"Come to the Science Institute's laboratory tomorrow," replied the young scientist, "and I will show you a document which, I'm sure, will very much interest you. Will we say 3 p.m.?"

"I'll be there—alone?"

"Yes please. Then, you can decide what revelations you can make to your mother."

People had calmed down. Leven finished his address, speaking with all the scientific passion which filled his soul. According to him, there were great sacrifices to be made, a great deal of work to be accomplished, but there was no doubt that the definitive exploration of Sumatra would yield its bold conquerors veritable triumphs, both in the scientific and commercial domains... But would there be men sufficiently venturesome to risk sufficient capital?

"Mr. Leven," a voice spoke up, "you forget that you belong to my firm, the Vanderheim Co., which should tell you that these bold men are already found... As early as tomorrow, the details of a new expedition, which we ask you to lead, will be mapped out, assuming you agree to expatriate yourself once more."

"Yes, yes," cried out the listeners. "He must return! He has no right to escape his duty."

"You see," said Vanderheim, "*vox populi, vox Dei!*"

Leven replied, smiling:

"Certainly, I do not reject *a priori* the honorable mandate which my country wishes me to undertake, but you will allow me, however, my dear employer, and all of you my good friends and compatriots, to think it over for a few days."

And he added, lowering his voice: "I may have to take care of a few personal matters."

"My dear scholar, take your time," replied Vanderheim. "Tomorrow, we'll discuss all the details, but for now, I ask Dr. Valtenius to take the floor. We, too, must, in our patriotic duty, assure Holland's glory in these possible discoveries."

"Certainly!" the doctor replied. "Ah! If I were but 20 years old, 30, 50! But 76…"

He broke off suddenly:

"Ha! Ha!" he said, rising to his feet, "who knows?"

Chapter III

Margaret and her mother had returned to their mansion in Hoogstraat in a state of great excitement. Once they were alone, Louisa, in tears, threw herself upon the sofa.

"Mother! Mother!" cried out the young girl, running to her and hugging her. "Why cry? Why these tears?"

"Ah! Dear child, how can it be that you have not understood? As I listened to this young man, I played over in my mind the terrible scene during which your brother, my darling George, disappeared... And I don't know what sort of crazy hope crossed my mind! Who knows if in that impenetrable wilderness, the description of which terrified me, my son, your brother, does still live?"

"Well! I must admit, mother, as I listened to him—Mr. Leven—a sort of involuntary hope rose in me."

"So you see!"

"And I regretted not being a man, not being able to undertake such heroic explorations."

"Really! You would wish to be involved in such an enterprise?"

Margaret looked at her mother. Yes, the thought had arisen in her, but did she dare express it?

At that moment, Wilhelm Villiers entered the room. Drawn on by an uncontrollable curiosity, he inquired about this exchange, the subject of which he could not help but be preoccupied about. His wife told him of the feelings she had experienced. Villiers listened to her patiently.

"I'm afraid," he said, "that our friend Mr. Leven is letting himself be drawn along by his passion for science. That the island of Sumatra contains much gold has long been established. However, when it comes to primitive races, close to humans, those are, I believe, worthless fantasies."

"But Dr. Valtenius seemed convinced."

"I don't deny that his opinion weighs in heavily, but he, too, might have succumbed to an impulse which will prove false upon mature reflection. As for our son, alas, my dear Luisa, you forget that ten years have passed since the catastrophe of Kota-Rajia... Can you pretend that, were he still alive, he would not have found some way to communicate with the inhabitants of Sumatra? He would be 20 years old now... Would you postulate him to be held in such captivity as to make it impossible for him to contact other men? This would be believing in more than a miracle. If this lecture awoke in you some painful delusions, I almost regret acceding to your wishes. Believe me, our George is truly lost to us forever. Besides, since Mr. Vanderheim is interested in these explorations, we will chat with Mr. Leven tomorrow, but everything will come down to commercial interests."

All night, Margaret was unable to sleep; some unexplained emotions troubled her. She, more than anyone, had reveled in the success of the one she had chosen deep in her heart to be her future husband. She had savored with delight the triumph afforded her by the young man's glances. Besides, she anxiously awaited the appointment the explorer had asked her to keep. In his tone, she had read something mysterious, and her heightened curiosity already suggested a number of hypotheses, which she accepted and rejected in turn.

At the approach of morning, at dawn, when, suc-
cumbing to her fatigue, she dropped off into a light
slumber, the dream which had already haunted her, again
took shape: there were the deep jungle, so thick that the
branches hid the sky, the huge trunks, forming an impenetrable enclosure around the clearing. In the half-light,
she saw strange outrageous bodies shifting about, creatures that bore the shape of men, but whose features she
could not make out. In the middle of them, she saw a
pale-faced, blond-haired young man, sitting atop a
mound and seemingly talking to them, like a professor
teaching his pupils.

The young man had George's features, as she remembered them from her childhood memories. Suddenly, amidst this deep peacefulness, a storm arose;
lightning broke through the tight canopy; the trees
snapped; a burst of wind raced through destroying everything in its way. Margaret saw the strange creatures drop
one by one, struck down by the lightning, and George
who remained alone, knelt beside a dead body and cried.

She woke with a start, horrified, and ran to her window. The daylight was coming, with that deliciously
softness of northern dawns. She breathed in deeply, tearing herself from the painful nightmare. After all, was it
not perfectly natural for last night's worries to raise such
visions in her brain? Were these not evoked by her sleep,
and without any ties to reality?

She ran to her mother, who, fortunately, had not
been disturbed by the same hauntings. On the contrary,
she had regained her composure and gave her daughter a
long hug, as if to prove to her that she was concentrating
all the love remaining in her heart upon her.

"You are at the same time my son and my daughter," she said. "Don't be jealous of the dear one we have lost, because I love him as reflected in you."

Margaret did not speak to her mother of the visit she had promised Leven. She found a pretext to go out with old Zabeth, her governess, in whose discretion she was assured.

When she reached the scientific institute, Leven was waiting for her. The young scientist quickly came up to her.

"Thank you for coming," he said. "Pardon me for having solicited this visit in a somewhat unconventional manner, but there are moments when secrecy is paramount, when certain revelations are so strange, so delicate, that only the bravest souls can withstand them."

He led her into one of the laboratory rooms. Arranged on a long table, all sorts of mineral samples were on display. From a carefully locked drawer, Leven drew out a rock, a sort of rounded and polished pebble.

"Listen to me, dear Margaret," he said in a voice trembling with emotion. "You trust me and do not believe me capable of playing on your deeply held emotions. Now, draw upon all your self-control and look at this stone."

He placed it in the young girl's hands. She examined it, then cried out. On the smooth surface two letters stood out, deeply carved, a G and a V.

"What's this?" she cried out. "Where is this stone from? What do these letters mean?"

"Does it not seem to you," said Leven softly, "that they are initials?"

"There's no doubt of that! But again, where was this stone found?"

"In the bed of a torrent that clearly has its origins in the central highlands of Sumatra. But, I beg you, examine the characters closely: they are rough and irregular; do they not seem to bear a personal component?"

Margaret had allowed herself to collapse onto a seat, so pale she seemed about to faint.

"G.V.," she muttered, "George Villiers!"

"Ah! Well I knew," exclaimed Leven, "that you would translate these two enigmatic letters as I do. But look more closely at them: is it not clear that they were traced out by a yet inexperienced hand, by the hand of a child?"

"Yes, that's for sure. When my brother disappeared, he was ten years old, and in Aceh, he had received only the most rudimentary of schooling."

"Don't forget," replied Leven, "that the natives know next to nothing of European alphabet; their writing comes from Sanskrit. Thus these letters cannot have been traced out by anyone else but a European. Now, this stone comes from a region where very few of our kinsmen have penetrated. How long had it tumbled down the torrent from which I picked it up by chance? Now you understand why I wished to show this to you and you alone."

"I thank you, as my mother's emotional response would have been so powerful that it might have killed her, especially since, after all, this isn't an absolute proof of my brother's survival. If it's possible, even probable, that these letters were carved by him, how long had that stone been sitting there where you picked it up?"

"I cannot answer that; however, there is there a clear indication that your brother didn't die immediately in the catastrophe which has been so often recounted. We must therefore return to the hypothesis that, due to circumstances which still escape us, he was led into the wilderness of Sumatra, and, one day, obeying some vague hope of indicating his existence, he carved out the two letters on this stone, which he then left to fate. When did he do this? That, we don't know. That's why I would not have wished to present your dear mother with such a precarious hope."

Margaret had regained her composure.

"Your discretion directed you well," she said, "and I'm infinitely grateful. I myself dare not hope that my brother is still alive, and yet... I don't doubt that it was my dear George who carved those letters... I want to believe—no, I believe that he is alive, but at the same time, I feel a most poignant sadness, thinking that I shall no doubt never see him again! And yet, what if such a miracle could occur, that the greatly loved and lamented son were to be returned to his mother? Alas, it is all but impossible."

Big tears formed in Margaret's eyes.

"Who knows?" said Leven. "Have you not heard that Mr. Vanderheim pledged himself to organize a new expedition. Certainly, it will be very costly, and it will be tiring work, but it would be planned in such a manner that a methodical search would deliver all of Sumatra's secrets to the explorers."

"Yes, I understand," said Margaret, shifting her hand over her heart, "and you are ready to take on this task? You will leave again... For years maybe... And I... I..."

She interrupted herself; she was crying.

Leven approached her, and took her hand, saying softly:

"Margaret, I, too, sense how painful this separation would be, and I'll tell you something more, I don't wish to force it upon myself."

"What do you mean?"

"Truly," continued Leven, "I'm greatly honored to have been chosen as the leader of the new expedition, whose scientific and commercial pursuits could bear huge dividends! But what is that compared to a lifetime of happiness... And my happiness is not in Sumatra, it is here! Say the word, Margaret, and I will turn down the position they wish to confer on me."

"Oh! No, don't do that!" cried out the young woman. "I have no right to tear apart your life. A great future presents itself to you, thanks to the confidence Mr. Vanderheim has in you, and which you so richly deserve. Think no more of me! I give you back your freedom."

"What if I refuse it? Margaret, listen to me! As you yourself have said, my employers' confidence in me imposes certain obligations which would be difficult for me to shirk. Nonetheless, I would be ready to refuse this assignment, but I feel I have another duty: to solve the life and death questions which lie hidden in the Malaysian wilderness. I want to know the truth, to know whether all hope of finding your brother should truly be abandoned. You see, I am torn between such widely scattered emotions that I don't dare decide one way or another. Yet, this I know, Margaret: I cannot live without you."

Margaret blushed with a feeling of deepest delight.

"Mr. Leven", she said, "if I understand you well, if you are thinking of refusing the mission Mr. Vanderheim has offered you, it is because you would be most distressed to leave me, to be separated from me..."

"A sadness so great that I don't think I'd have the strength to bear it."

"Who tells you that I could bear it?"

"Margaret!"

"I, in turn, will tell you that I have no right to keep you here, not only because your entire future is linked with this expedition, but even more so because, as long as the faintest hope of finding my beloved brother exists, it would be criminal to give up now... So I beg you to go."

"What do you mean?"

"If memory serves," said Margaret smiling, "the law says that a wife must follow her husband everywhere."

"Go on!"

"Go ask my father for my hand in marriage, and I will obey the law!"

"Ah! How good you are to me and how I love you! But do I have the right to take hold of your life, to expose you to the strains and dangers which await us?"

"I am strong and courageous, and I shall be worthy of you. Must I not also sacrifice myself for my brother's sake?"

At that very moment, the laboratory's door opened and Dr. Valtenius appeared on the threshold, his head uncovered, his hair tousled:

"I can't stand it!" he cried out. "I haven't slept all night! All I dreamt of were apes that were men and who mocked my ignorance. Mr. Leven, when you leave for Sumatra, will you allow me to accompany you? I know I'm not 20 any more, but I'm still hearty, solid on my feet and clear-sighted... Yes, I'm 76, but one could say that's only twice 38. Tell me you accept!"

"Wholeheartedly, my dear Doctor," said Leven squeezing both his hands in his own, "however, I would ask you for a couple of days' grace."

"All right, but don't delay too much. At my age, you know, one can't wait too long. What the Devil keeps us here?"

"A most important reason," said Leven laughing, "I only ask you leave me time to marry. May I introduce you to my future wife!"

"You are to wed Miss Villiers? Good, very good! Well, that's your business. I'm not saying you're wrong to do so, but, please, hurry up!"

Chapter IV

A few days later, a mysterious scene played itself out in another part of Rotterdam.

There was on the shore of the Haringvliet, near the Old West bridge, an inn of ill repute called *The Black Lion*. It was a den of out of work sailors, deserters, the dregs of adventurers, which, in sea ports, make up a community open to giving a hand in any enterprise, even criminal ones.

That night, a tall man, wrapped in a black overcoat and wearing an oversized hat which hid his features, entered the inn by a back door. The innkeeper, a stout, gnome-like creature, who had had numerous scrapes with the law, was both in the confidence of and accomplice to all the illegal undertakings which were commonplace to his clients. He bowed deeply to the man and led him to a private salon, off the common room where the drunkards were mixing loudly.

"Your lordship is early," the innkeeper said, "but Captain Ned should be here any minute. I know that boy, he's punctuality personified."

"Very well," said the stranger. "Bring a bottle of gin and two glasses. Then, as soon as the man arrives, bring him in here. Above all, be careful. Keep in mind that the least indiscretion will cost you dearly... And you know that if I reward well those who serve me, I also know how to punish those who betray me."

"Don't worry, I know my people," said the innkeeper. "You're among those one doesn't want to rub the wrong way. Besides, here's your man. I'll make sure nobody bothers you."

He slipped aside to allow the one named Captain Ned to enter. He was a real old salt, with a burnished face; a short beard covered all of his lower face and sideburns.

The gin having been brought, the two men were alone.

"Well, Captain, have you succeeded?" asked the stranger.

"Excellently, Mr. Koolman, you will be pleased."

"No need to say my name here. So you've understood, I need 50 strong, determined men, strapping fellows who will not back down from any task."

"Fifty villains!" stated Ned simply.

Koolman—such was his name—grimaced slightly.

"You're rather blunt," he said, "let us rather say, adventurers. In short, have you able to collect such a crew?"

"Done! I chose them myself. One could search all the prisons in Europe and not come up with better!"

Koolman held back a gesture of impatience; the other man's bluntness annoyed him. Truly, just as much as Captain Ned's face spoke of a frank, impudent roguery, exhibiting a sort of brutal handsomeness, so was Koolman's face equally tainted by the stigmata of vulgarity and hypocrisy. One could expect no less of him than lies and double-crosses. He was clean-shaven, sallow-hued, ugly, and shifty-eyed.

"And these men are ready to ship out?"

"Absolutely—ready as soon as I pay them their agreed upon advance of 100 florins per head."

"Good, I will give you the money."

He drew from his pocket a wallet swollen with bills.

"Just a minute," Ned spoke up. "Before we wrap up, I need to talk to you, to ask you to give me some details about certain things."

Koolman nearly jumped out of his seat; the tone of these words had greatly angered him.

"Details?" he replied. "Well! Captain, you seem to think a great deal of yourself; undoubtedly you forget that one word from me and you're lost."

"I know that full well, Mr. Koolman. I know all too well that I am in your power, because of that damn counterfeiting scheme I was so stupid to tell you about."

"And to supply me with the proof, remember that!"

"Yes, yes, I know, I'm a loser, I don't disagree, but at least, I have an excuse. Hounded by bad luck, I've pursued every trade and have succeeded in none. Were I to wish to become an honest man again, I couldn't. It's actually the only career that isn't open to me. But this is not about me, but about you."

"About me?"

"Well, yes. If I'm a crook, one can account for that. I have no other trade, but you, Mr. Koolman, can't use that excuse."

"What are you saying? You dare!"

"I allow myself to believe that if Mr. Koolman, a former partner of the Vanderheim Co., with a fortune of hundreds of thousands of florins, invites Capt.ainNed, a gallows-bird, to recruit on his behalf a crew of former or future convicts, it isn't only to bounce a few ideas off them. I suspect that it's to have them commit one or more crimes, and so I have reason to be surprised. It's not clear to me what's going on here, and I like to know what I'm getting into. So, Mr. Koolman, before wrapping up and putting my friends at your disposal I want to know where we're going, why we are leaving, and more or less what our assignment will consist of."

"Truly you're most impudent! And if I were to refuse to answer?"

"I would tell you to keep your money, and I would keep my men, you understand. This is not a pang of conscience—that's something I'm long cured of—but let's say for example that one Mr. Koolman, for some doubtful speculation or other, wished to make a killing by taking out insurance on a ship that would then go down at sea... It's been done, and it pays well!"

"I swear that it's nothing like that!" exclaimed Koolman.

"I could list a number of other schemes just as compromising to the health of the crew, but that would lead us too far afield. If it is nothing like that, tell me what it's all about."

Koolman thought for a moment:

"Why not, after all? I have too much of a hold on you for you to turn on me. What I want to do is, take revenge on Vanderheim's firm!"

"A former partner's grudge... Things are getting clearer. And what the Devil did the Vanderheims do to you? You used to be such good friends."

"And now we're enemies, bitter enemies. They humiliated me, expressed their suspicions regarding my honesty."

"Impossible," replied Ned, in a serious tone which the ironic twist of his lips belied.

"They insolently criticized my management methods, when I was directing our colonial business with energy and a steady hand."

"Ah, yes!" Ned interrupted again, "that story of 200 Malays gassed in a cave."

111

"What I want to do is, take revenge on Vanderheim's firm!"

"They played the humanitarians! Those idiots think that you can handle those brutes like men, and since I refused to listen to their squalling, they turned the board of directors and the stockholders against me. I was forced to resign. Well, Ned, I vowed to make them pay dearly for the affronts I have suffered, and that's why I need you."

"Bravo!" cried out Ned. "Now that that's out, it's crystal clear! Good—honest hatred explains everything."

"And I feel that hatred in my heart for the Vanderheims, and for that damn Villiers, the so-called 'honest man,' my greatest adversary. Oh! I'll find a way to avenge myself on him too. So, under these conditions, can I count on you?"

"Absolutely! My men and I are all yours! But, tell me, what will your role be in all of this?"

"I will be your leader, undeclared, of course."

"You will leave with us?"

"No, but I will reach our destination at the same time, and according to the circumstances, I will act."

"All right, and where are we going?"

"To Sumatra!"

"A lovely country where there are fortunes to be made."

"And where I want the Vanderheims to come to ruin. Do you know the country?"

"Damn sure! I served there during the conquest. How many of those Malays and Aceh did I kill! How many of those Sakays and Battaks did I hunt down!"

"It will be for such hunting that I will use you. By the way, when is the *Borean*, which is to take the Leven expedition to Malaysia, due to leave?"

"On behalf of the Vanderheims! Ha ha! Now I begin to understand! It is against that scientist and his team that we will have to act."

"Perhaps. One way or the other, I demand complete secrecy."

"Relax, I just wanted to have a clear picture—light has been shed and I'm your man. So, to answer your question, the *Borean* leaves in 10 days, this delay being necessary for the marriage of Mr. Leven with Margaret Villiers. So Leven will soon be your enemy's son-in-law. Everything's coming together! This could be fun!"

"You talk too much! Mind your own business. Here are 5000 florins for your men, plus 5000 for you, I leave the *Porpoise* in your hands."

"Ah! The nice little steamer? Now there's one that sails like the wind."

"First thing tomorrow, you'll board and supply the ship. You will register for Malacca, with ports of call along the coast of Sumatra. Of course, I don't appear anywhere in any of this; the steamer is rented in your name, and you're in charge of everything."

"And when do we leave?"

"Twenty-four hours before the *Borean*, whose progress will be slower, which will allow you to outstrip it by two days. You will put in at Banda Aceh and will wait for me there."

"OK! You can count on me!"

And Ned held out his open hand to Koolman, who put his hand in it, with a wry face.

Leven and Margaret's marriage had taken place. Villiers and Luisa had accepted this painful sacrifice, without the youngsters revealing all their hopes. And, on the date set, the young couple went aboard the *Borean* with Peter Villiers, the chemist, Margaret's uncle.

A few minutes before departure, a man ran onto the deck. It was Dr. Valtenius crying out: "Wait! You're not going to forget me! Don't leave me behind!"

None knew that their enemies had already gone out ahead, the night before, on the *Porpoise*.

Part Three: In Aapland

Chapter I

As the preceding scenes played out in Europe, what had happened in the mysterious island since the dark hours when George Villiers had been carried off through mountains and forests, into a territory unknown and as yet unexplored by man?

One must remember that, barely 50 years ago, maps of Africa showed extensive blank regions labeled with the discouraging legend: "*Unexplored.*"

Is it therefore not surprising that, if lands adjoining Europe had remained unexplored, those of the Asian islands, thousands of leagues away, had remained closed to the explorations of travelers, barely bold enough to adventure themselves on their shores. Besides, these islands were fiercely defended by barbaric peoples fighting to maintain their independence.

Of the island of Sumatra, the coasts were known: Aceh, Lohong, Edi, Deli, Siak, and, to the south, Padany, Benkoelen, Rangsang situated across from Singapore, and Palembang separated from the tip of the island of Krakatoa by a sort of desert and the straits of Sund.

But the great mountain range—the island's spine—extending along the western coast, but branching out into the interior by way of secondary ranges, demarcating vast cirques, piles of boulders, impenetrable thickets, remained unexplored. Today, the region remains protected against the incursion of Europeans by an unexplained and terrible fear.

The foothills bore evidence of the violence of massive eruptions, where lands of Tertiary origin, from before the advent of man, had emerged as a result of the fiery subterranean activity, drawn from the very bowels of the planet. Above the original range, which seldom exceeded 1200 meters in altitude, further upheavals of untold magnitude had raised volcanic cones, whose sleeping craters remain suspended at nearly 4000 meters in altitude, an eternal menace hanging over the ever imperiled island. Six of these fiery mouths still rumble and bubble, as if to remind one of their terrible origins. Such are Korindji and Kaba, from which large lava flows continually run, as well as Radja Bas which, through its subterranean outlets, branches out into the Straits, and whose anger one day led to the terrible Krakatoa disaster.

Before these terrible guardians, even the boldest hesitate. How many have risked their lives to tear fits dark secrets from the Malaysian island, but have never returned? Or who have, perhaps maddened with fear, painted such horrifying pictures that none dared follow in their footsteps. Were they to be believed when they claimed that central Sumatra was defended by legions of strange demons, legendary denizens of prehistoric times?

Were these a race predating Ptolemy's ancient Jabadin, ignored by Marco Polo, who visited the island at the end of the 13th century? How had they survived? How had they resisted the invasions of all the Oriental races which, according to the geographers, had met at this crossroad of Asia's land and sea route: Hindus and Tamils from India, Chinese, Boughis, Arabs, Javanese and Sundanese from Java, Indonesians and Malays, Mongols and Koubons, Kassims and Battas?

In actuality, nobody had seen these quasi-mythological creatures, which some claimed were terrible giants, and others stated were wispy as phantoms, the seeds of nightmare escaped from some Buddhist Hell. The monstrous, grinning, triple-bodied, multi-limbed deities were well guarded: man-eating tigers; rhinoceros; huge elephants, capable with their feet of crushing a man's head like a ripe fruit; panthers leaping, striking and slinking away with their prey; marauding snakes, whose slithery movement barely drew a rustle from the leaves and branches; while in the tree canopy, suddenly on the defensive, the green-breasted red-beaked *gongog* served as lookout and announced man's approach to all his enemies.

However, the lust for profit is the mother of daring and recklessness. Since the Dutch conquest, under the pretext of civilization and an insatiable appetite for wealth, adventurers had tried storming this central fortress, defended by Nature from invaders. Some studies, rather superficial as yet, but relatively accurate, had revealed the existence of exploitable deposits of tin, mercury, and especially, gold! That very word—gold— excited the most timid, and already a number of expeditions had been organized and crowned with relative success.

The bait was two-fold: not only the existence of nuggets carried by the torrents, but early prospecting of gold-bearing veins, indicated the existence of natural treasures. However, some curious facts had also been ascertained. Beneath some monoliths, whose shape and size recalled those in Brittany and Stonehenge, depositories of gold had been discovered, like some cache where

117

primitive men would have buried, hidden, hoarded, miser-like, large quantities of the precious metal. The explorers had recognized, without the shadow of a doubt, that these great stone masses had been lifted, moved and put back in place by human hands. One had seen no traces of tools, or at least their role had only been secondary. It was by sheer muscle- power—and what workers must have undertaken this strenuous work!—that these huge stones had been hoisted onto the narrowest of ridges, to the most difficult locations.

But what was inexplicable,—one recalls that Frederik Leven, in his presentation, had alluded to these circumstances—was that, after having recognized the presence of the gold, but before they had had the leisure to return to collect it with men and machines, the prospectors had no longer found the anticipated treasures at the site, but rather a shapeless and viscous mud. All that was said was:

"It is dead gold!"

And the popular imagination, taking up the expression, had completed the story by attributing this destruction of the gold, this assassination of the king of metals, to the mysterious creatures whose diabolical resistance defied all human efforts—the Gold Destroyers!

The scientists exhausted themselves in unusual explanations. They believed neither in prehistoric monsters, nor in gold destroyers, but, to save face, they attributed the unique phenomenon of the gold's destruction to the influence of the torrid Sun and superheated air—which, stated in a serious tone, made much sense, but in truth had none.

What, then, was this mysterious world? This is what we know.

One will not have forgotten that, after the brutal battle with the Maouass, To-Ho's tribe had pushed on into the depths of the mountainous landscape, taking along young George, who had once again lost consciousness.

It was entirely impossible for him to have the least notion of the places he was traveling through. A powerful fever had declared itself and, in this frail organism, the disease progressed so rapidly—as he had since found out—that they had thought him at risk of dying.

After how long had he regained consciousness? One morning, he had opened his eyes and had immediately closed them, so much the first scene which presented itself seemed strange, like a nightmare vision. He was stretched out on a raised bed made of leaves and branches, prone on the hamac-like couch which lianas held, a foot off the ground, to two tree trunks.

Near him, standing up, was a creature greatly resembling a ape—or, to be more accurate, a she-ape—who, upon the movement he had made, suddenly bent over, watching him with her large wide-open eyes. Large as a woman, massive, heavy-set, she was perfectly hideous, yet in the curve of her thick lips, in her eyes, was a such a compelling sign of gentleness and kindness that George, his first surprise past, was not scared and began to smile.

A rather sad smile nonetheless, since this poor boy had passed through such terrible ordeals that he was but a shade of his former self. He was white as wax and his wide eyes were sunken in below his brow. Instinctively, he said:

"Drink!"

He wasn't yet able to reason, or else he would have been somewhat surprised that, upon the syllable being

119

spoken—*drinken*—one must not forget that the young Villiers spoke only Dutch—the she-ape, without a single moment's hesitation, dropped her head in a sign of assent, and, leaving the enclosure for an instant, quickly returned, bearing a sort of funnel made from a smooth, emerald-green leaf.

It contained a colorless liquid, water no doubt. She brought it close to his lips and he drank. A delicious taste tickled his palate, and childlike, he continued:

"*Gut!*" [16]

She truly laughed this time, and repeated—not *gut*!—but a syllable which comprised only the sound *gue*, with a silent ending, something like *gue, gue*, the *e* being little stressed.

He took no notice and spoke up again:

"Thank you, you're very nice... Tell me, where am I?"

She bent over him, all the muscles of her face tightening in a great effort. Her ear was bent into a conch shape, as though to smell out in some way the sounds proffered her. But it was clear that she did not understand him. He became impatient, speaking faster and louder:

"Who are you? I want to get up, leave here... Why do you look at me like that, instead of answering me? My! How ugly you are!"

He had cried out nastily, in a rage, perhaps to force his interlocutrix from her calm front, for she still watched him with the same good-willed, attentive, and especially curious look, but she spoke not a syllable more.

So, exasperated, he stiffened in his hamac, grabbed hold of the supporting lianas, and tried to raise himself,

---

[16] Good!

but she held him back, well knowing that he had not the strength to get down, and that he would fall. She placed both hands on his shoulders, forcing him to lie back down

But he did not wish to. In a fit of anger, such as children are prone to, he tried to push away the arm which held him back, but he might as well have attacked a steel bar. Exasperated, he bit her finger to the blood. She made a small cry, drew back her hand and looked at it. As a red drop hung on her brown hairs, she gave out a reproachful *ho!* but not in anger. She slipped her head through a gap in the shelter and called out in one long syllable something like *ho-o-o-o-k.*

The boy, perhaps tired out by his outburst of anger, reclined again, with that vague fear of punishment that haunts children. Having understood that the she-ape had called for help, he looked wide-eyed at the doorway through which he expected her avenger to appear. Someone did appear: another ape, this one so ugly that George could not hold back a shiver of fear. Now, shaking in fear, he sank back into his bed of mosses, as if he wished to drown himself in it.

This creature resembled neither To-Ho, nor his female companion. First of all, he was smaller, less square shouldered, more comparable to a man in his stature, but what distinguished him most of all was the color of his skin, which was not brown, but a pasty yellowish-white. He was not naked; he wore about his loins a sort of skirt, and sandals made of lianas on his feet. He was uncovered above the waist; the chest thin, emaciated, ribs protruding, and, at the end of a very long, muscular neck, stood a large bald-topped head, with a crown of spikes of white hair.

The face, of an indefinite hue, brick and white ground together, was furrowed with tiny wrinkles, so fine, so numerous, that not one spot, be it the nose, the cheeks, or the brow were free of them. The eyelids themselves, which fell heavily and half hid his eyes, were flabby and creased. The discolored lips no longer made up a distinct line and the chin disappeared beneath a heavy, shaggy, yellowish-white beard. Upon seeing this mask, comical in its hideousness, George had trouble holding back nervous laughter, and his initial worry shifted to an insurmountable urge to burst out laughing.

The strange ape approached his bed and said to him in the finest Dutch: "We do not wish you any harm!"

As the newcomer entered the hut, the she-ape exchanged a few guttural monosyllabic and incomprehensible words with him, but which must have had some meaning, since he listened attentively, nodded his head in the manner of a man, and finally, after having looked at the she-ape's injured hand, softly patted her on the shoulder, inviting her to retire.

George saw that he was to remain alone with this grotesque gnome, and, again, terror overcame him.

"No! No!" he cried out, "I don't want to... Please Mrs. Monkey, stay! I beg you! I won't be naughty anymore! Please stay!"

But she had already disappeared, and as the boy burrowed into the hamac, terrified, the strange ape approached his bed and said to him in the finest Dutch:

"Now, little one, you must behave yourself. We do not wish you any harm! Don't worry, I tell you, you have nothing to fear from me or anyone here. You have been sick, but you have been well cared for. Now that you are out of danger, you must be well behaved and grateful, accommodate yourself to the life—most happy—one lives in this country, and if I live long enough, I will teach you all I have learned—the science of peace and happiness."

Chapter II

George was flabbergasted. This ape spoke his language! His surprise was such that, at first, he could think of nothing to say in reply. The ape had a weak, somewhat hoarse voice, but softened it as much as he could. Little by little, George came to be reassured, now looking at this wrinkled face, the puffy eyes, the pale mouth, in a sort of commiseration.

"Let's see," continued the other, "do you feel you have the strength to get up? Don't be afraid! Come into my arms, hold on to my neck. I am quite old, but I have saved my strength for so long that there remains enough to carry you."

Not knowing why, the boy obeyed him. He put his two arms around his neck, and the other, taking him in his arms, lifted him from his hamac.

He carried him outside, stepped over the stone enclosure surrounding the hut, climbed a path through some bushes and reached a lush green plateau crowned with huge palm trees. There, on the thick carpet of grass, he put the child down.

George staggered. The other supported him. Then, with a circular hand motion, he said to him:

"Look, is it not truly beautiful?"

The view was indeed marvelous: all around them a vast circle spread out, dominated in the rear by jagged rocks upon which the sunlight, very soft, as if filtered, added blue and violet reflections. Below, in a deep forested valley, were great expanses of trees—mangoes, grapefruit, bamboos and *loukoums*—which, in foreground and background, arranged in a number of picturesquely irregular terraces, created a truly dreamlike landscape. From all this abundant Nature, full of life, of greenery, of light, emanated a placid aroma. The air, charged with balsamic odors, as if saturated with all of the Earth's emanations, filled the nostrils, the lungs, with a deep sense of life. The sky displayed rare and delicate hues, giving the impression of endless vistas, and great flocks of birds passed over in elegant silhouettes outlined on the pale background. Halfway up the valley, on an almost bald-pated peak, whose only crown was one of mosses, was the splotch of a small steel-colored lake.

George stayed still, half recumbent in the grass, laying up on his elbow. It was as if he were hypnotized by this exquisite and engaging vista. He forgot everything, his fears, his anger, his surprise, to experience within himself—after the trials which had so shaken him—a most deeply felt sense of pleasure.

This comfort was such, so invasive and exquisite, that involuntarily he extended his hand to the old ape-man who spoke Dutch so well, and said to him:

"I've been naughty; you must forgive me."

The other placed a hand on his brow—a dry, wrinkled, ridged hand whose touch was nonetheless very delicate—and, smiling at the Sun, the trees, at nature, burst out laughing. Then, in a burst of curiosity, George asked:

"Please tell me where I am and who you are. You know, I'm not afraid of monkeys."

"I am a man," replied the other. "I used to be called—Oh, it was so long ago—Ludwig Van Kock, and I lived in Rotterdam."

"Rotterdam! Why, that's where I myself was born."

"Really? And your name is?"

"George Villiers."

"I once knew a family of that name... Let's see, tell me your story, up until the day when To-Ho—I know all about that—tore your from a frightful death and brought you here, poor orphan that you are."

Tears rose in George's eyes:

"Orphan? Yes... If you only knew! The Aceh killed my father, mother, and my little sister! It was frightful; we were in a whirlwind of steel and fire."

"Among men!" said Van Kock shaking his head. "Tell me everything. I will then tell you my story, but most of all, do not tire yourself!"

George then, in a rather incoherent manner—accuracy not being the purview of children—told as best he could the terrible adventures he had survived. For him, none of the details were fixed; from the time the Aceh had taken his mother, an incomprehensible nightmare had haunted his brain. All his thoughts were confused, the sudden arrival of his father seemed like a dream! His memories, the scenes which had played out before him, were tangled, mixed up together in a series of cries, explosions, fire, and blood!

He had seen men in their death throes drop around him, screaming women; his father, his mother, Margaret, had disappeared in a furnace. He didn't even know who had grabbed and taken him away.

The scene where To-Ho had appeared, and hurled his abductor into the abyss, had impressed him with naught but a sense of delirium, then nothing more until his first awakening in the forest, when he had felt the claws of the *maouass*, the ape against which the other had defended him—another ape, was it not?

"If it is of To-Ho which you speak, child, he is more than an ape, yet less than a man—but still better than a man."

"I don't understand!"

Just as Van Kock was about to answer, a sound of rapid footsteps sounded on the plateau and To-Ho appeared. In spite of himself, George cringed. It was because, in truth, To-Ho, by his broad-shouldered vigor, by all the strength which emanated from him, was frightening. Clearly, strong anger stirred him, as a tremor ran through all his limbs and his drawn-back lips showed, in a bestial grin, his menacing fangs.

Van Kock quickly interposed himself:

"To-Ho!" he said to him. "What's wrong with you? You look furious! You know that I have forbidden you to get angry."

He spoke to him in Dutch, but in a certain manner, emphasizing the vowels, stressing what one might term the backbone of the word. Clearly, this was an abbreviated language, primitive in a way, very difficult to render in writing.

To-Ho listened, and certainly understood.

He made a violent gesture, pointing out a location in the valley from whence guttural laugh-like cries rose, and cried out:

"*Dreka!*"

"Again?" said Van Kock angrily. "Ah! The wretches! The fools!"

Here is the explanation of the word *Dreka*. The Dutch word *Drunkaard* means drunk or drunkard. With great difficulty, Van Kock had managed to teach To-Ho and a few of his fellow ape-men not complete words, which they could not pronounce, but the basic underlying sounds.

Dreka—by way of the *dr* and the *k*—was the skeleton of the word *drunkaard*. To-Ho spoke the consonants and followed them by a short hammered out vowel. Thus had an intelligible language developed little by little between him and Van Kock. For example, figuring out all of sudden, in the forest, that little George must be hungry, he had spoken the word *Ete*—which is the root of the verb *Eten*, to eat.

Similarly, To-Ho's mate, Waa, had clearly understood the words *drinken*, to drink, and *gut*, good, as pronounced by the child. But in trying to repeat them she said *Dreka*—or *Gue*.

Thus Van Kock had made up from scratch a monosyllabic idiom which he had taught To-Ho and the other inhabitants of this mysterious country. This understood, we will translate into clear terms the speech and gesturing which accompanied each of the To-Ho pronouncements:

"Yes, yes, over there," he said. "I sneaked up on them; they are drunk on palm wine, and then there's gold!"

Gold is called *Goud* in Dutch, and he said: *Go* and, oddly enough, this word was not mistaken for *Gue*, the translation of *gut*, good. It is thus that in primitive languages, very small differences in pronunciation result in profound changes in meaning.

"Gold!" cried out Van Kock. "Ah! That is the enemy. It will destroy your race! It will destroy you to the last! Come, come, To-Ho!"

He had taken To-Ho by the arm.

"What about the little one?" said To-Ho, pointing at George. "We cannot leave him here alone."

He called out:

"Waa! Waa!"

She who had seemed no more than an ugly she-ape to George, ran up. To-Ho spoke to her rapidly, no longer in pseudo-Dutch, but in a special language, semi-animal so to speak, made up of grunts and short cries.

He told her:

"Waa! Take the child! Watch over him well, as you would have our poor little one, our own, the one killed by men."

Waa drew closer to George who, by instinct, held on to Van Kock.

"Go, child," he said. "She is your friend, your protector, she loves you and will love you more each day."

He pushed him into Waa's arms; her simian features lit up with a remarkable glow of goodwill and love. Mixed with the goodness in her big eyes were tears, for she remembered. She too had had a child, a son, almost of George's age, named To-Ho-Ti, or Ho-Ti by those close to him. She loved him, as mothers, human or beast, know how to love. Then, one day, reckless as he was, tearing through the forests and over the mountains, climbing with a marvelous agility the most dangerous peaks, the deepest gorges, defying the wild beasts and even fighting venomous snakes, he had gotten lost. He had run, bounded along for days on end, and, after this wild race, had fallen among a group of prospectors, adventurers in a quest for gold.

One of these men had sighted him over the end of his gun, and the child had dropped like a stone. To-Ho, mad with sorrow and worry, had searched long, and one day, had found his remains, which he had recognized. Nearby, he found the clear traces of men having spent some time there. Man! This creature was as mysterious to him as he was to them. To-Ho had wanted to better know his son's killers and had risked himself as far as their huts, their villages, their cities.

One of these men had sighted him over the end of his gun, and the child had dropped like a stone.

Thus had he reached the Aceh country, the very doors of Kota-Rajia, and it was there that he had been captured, turned over to Sultan Mahmoud, struck, tortured. But mostly, he had seen, he had pondered, with all the attention he could muster, this race of creatures which resembled him, but were yet so different from him in their barbaric fury and refined cruelty.

Truly, when the Aceh sovereign fustigated or lacerated his flesh, he could understand nothing of this need to do evil, nor could he see anything in the savage battle between people of the same race, who differed only in color. These creatures, which struck him as more clever and more delicate than he, even superior to him, at the same time presented themselves before him as nightmarish demons.

Certain details had struck him. In the Aceh Sultans' mausoleum, everything was dripping with gold and jewels, and To-Ho remembered Van Kock's teachings: gold was the enemy. It was to conquer it that men—for these people were called men—sought to penetrate into the mountain, to violate the *Aaps*' last refuge—this was the name Van Kock had given him, *Aap* meaning ape in Dutch—it was the gold-hunters who had killed his son!

Then, for the first time, To-Ho had understood why Van Kock, this fugitive from humanity, who had lived for years and years among them, in that splendid and generous landscape, had identified gold as the enemy against which they must fight, which had to be destroyed at all cost.

For the sake of the Aaps' survival, as soon as a vein was discovered, it had to be destroyed. Van Kock, a brilliant chemist, who, at the age of 20, disdaining his countrymen's hateful ignorance, had disappeared, was deemed dead. But, in reality, he had come to settle and live among these primitive creatures, and had made himself their teacher and defender.

The great scientific breakthrough of Aapland was the destruction of gold. Van Kock, retracing in reverse the work of the ancient alchemists, who had sought the philosopher's stone, the key to making gold, had found a way to destroy it instead. He had taught his methods to To-Ho, and we shall see them put to the test.

From this incursion among men—who had mistreated, chained and lashed him—To-Ho had mastered the concept that Van Kock spoke the truth: that men only lived, breathed, argued among themselves, and killed one another for one reason: gold. The sultan lacerating his limbs, striking with his gold-handled blade, bearing a golden diadem on his brow, golden necklaces about his neck, a golden belt about his hips, the walls of the mosque decorated in gold, fabrics, banisters, grillwork, paneling, all dripping with gold. The chiefs who obeyed the Sultan wore gold helmets; the sabers which served them to murder were encrusted with gold. Gold everywhere! Always gold! And with it, around it, through it, bloodshed, suffering, death!

To-Ho, while watching the frightful pageant of these officers, soldiers, and executioners from his iron cage, thought of his beloved solitudes back there, of his Sun, his trees, his flowers, and a horror of gold's chosen race, the human race, ingrained itself in him. He had viewed the final storm of the battle between the Aceh and the Dutch as a great manifestation of the evils of gold, and his hatred of men and disgust for the vile metal had only grown stronger.

It went as far as Igli-Otou, who wished to kill little George, a child—of roughly the same age as To-Ho's—and who wore gold bracelets on his wrists and ankles! Why had To-Ho saved the child of this cursed race? By instinct. Because the creature was weak and in the clutches of one far stronger, because some sort of intuition told him that Waa, the desolate mother, might be happy to rediscover the illusion of motherhood.

And he had foreseen well, since Waa now extended her arms to George. How she had nursed him! How she had obeyed old Kock, not sleeping, devoting herself day and night to the little creature, which she addressed in whispers by the name of her dear little lost one, Ho-Ti.

But George had not yet entirely given himself over to her; his human vanity resisted her simian affection. He remembered his mother, so charming in her soft blondness, so delicate and gracious. He looked at Waa's enormous paws, and, in spite of himself, compared them to the tiny hands which used to caress him.

"Do give her a hug, child," Van Kock told him. "Don't you see she's dying for you to do so?"

George still hesitated; then, like a sovereign condescending to have a subject come up to him, extended his forehead to Waa, who sobbing, deliriously happy, wrapped him in her arms and took him away clutched to her chest, repeating to him "*Ete! Ete!*"

Knowingly, she promised him something to eat, knowing that he must be famished.

Chapter III

Meanwhile, To-Ho and Van Kock descended towards the valley. Almost a centenarian, Van Kock still alert and full of vigor, all bone and muscle, followed his companion through the trees and rocks.

Van Kock was quite a strange individual, one whom a bout of anger and misanthropy had thrown into a life in the wilds. Being Dutch, he was passionate, full of enthusiasm, and had given himself wholeheartedly to the study of chemistry and the natural sciences. His way of thinking had led him to the boldest speculations: he had studied the ancient alchemists in detail, and contrary to so many so-called research scientists, who speak of the alchemists' works without knowing them, he had gone back to the original texts, had had the courage to brave the enormous folios of Paracelsus, of Raymond Lulle, of Bernard de Trévisan, and of Arnaud de Villeneuve; he had read Artephius' *Natural Philosophy*, Crosset de la Haumerie's *Hidden Secrets of Cosmogeny*, and had spent days and nights pouring over the *Emerald Tables* attributed to Hermes, and, little by little, certain singular conclusions had impressed themselves upon his mind.

To him, Nature arose from unity: the primordial substance was unique, bearing within itself all power and motion, and, by its evolving nature, had created all that exists, those things inorganic as well as those living, the latter emerging from the former under the action of an unceasing progression of the primordial substance. What was surprisingly diverse and varied in appearance were only successive steps in a natural progression.

From gas to mineral, then to plants, on to animals, and finally to man, the progression was uninterrupted. Kock did not believe in the direct metamorphosis of stone into plant life, nor that of plant into animal life, but believed that the work undertaken by the primordial substance had taken on a concrete form in the mineral state, and then, having achieved this, stepped back, so to speak, to take a new leap forward, at the end of which it reached a higher state.

Thus, between ape and man, it was only the missing link that interested him. Nature's forward thrust had, according to him, created the ape; the workmanship was not perfect, so it had stepped back, had thrown itself forward again... Had it then, in this second leap, reached as far as man? Notwithstanding their analogous anatomies, he could not admit to it, so large were the differences between the two life-forms. He had then set forth the theory that the work of Nature must have produced, in its successive forward thrusts, creatures more and more distinct from the ape, evolving more and more towards man, and which had existed—or might still exist—as an evolutionarily fixed species.

Did they exist? Therein did the problem lie. When one observes nowadays the disappearance of entirely human races—such as the Native Americans—driven off, hunted down, and massacred by the Americans; when one sees the day to day demise of animal species such as the bison, to the point where costly attempts are being made to save the few remaining specimens, can one reasonably expect that creatures akin to man would have escaped the attacks of a conqueror who, by the right of his newly developed intelligence, has become master of the Earth and is used to doing away with his rivals?

Nonetheless, if some specimens of such pre-human races had survived, then the old legends probably bore some basis in reality, however twisted by ignorance or embellished by the imagination they might be. This theory had long ago been stated by the philosopher Ephemerus. Van Kock had made it his own: giants and monsters had indeed committed the heinous crimes attributed them in mythological history, and had been destroyed by men whom public gratitude had raised to the rank of demi-god. But driven back, driven away from civilized lands, would there not have been some which would have taken refuge in the impenetrable hinterlands?

And so, at 20 years of age, Van Kock, in his scientific fervor, had come to explore the island of Sumatra. While his countrymen dreamt only its economic potential, of the riches to be found, he, inspired by the few legends which had reached Europe, had, in an act of laudable daring, taken on the mission of exploring those regions where no one had yet penetrated.

He had returned to his country having seen, with his own eyes, creatures which represented a link between the simian and human races. He stated it, presenting his arguments, his proof. Then, among the scientific community, the civil servants, the middle-class, in the research institutes, among all those who exploit existing knowledge and systematically reject anything which might trouble their serenity and force them to further study, a great cry of indignation had arisen. He was called an ignoramus, a liar, even a heretic; he was anathematized from the scientific community.

*Van Kock, in his scientific fervor, had come to explore
the island of Sumatra.*

Did he not deny creation as it was explained in the
Bible? But there was more: he was rich. His family denounced him as mad and had him declared incompetent;
had themselves appointed as his legal guardians. The
lust for gold completed the work begun by ignorance
and intolerance. He was dishonored, singled out in public, ruined, and threatened with internment in a lunatic
asylum.

Then, disgusted with man, with his stupidity, his
narrow-mindedness and greediness, knowing that his
arrest was only hours away, Van Kock had escaped, and,
using up his last monetary resources, had embarked on a
ship under an assumed name. Having arrived in Sumatra,

and having miraculously escaped the dangers represented by the natives' hatred for Europeans, he had made his way into the forests, had hiked for weeks and months through the mountains, climbing the most inaccessible of peaks, defending himself against the wild beasts, and finally he had fallen in with a tribe of anthopoids.

There again, the danger was great, as amongst these creatures, then more akin to the ape than to man, an instinct of ferocious brutality predominated. But an unexpected circumstance had saved him. He had cured To-Ho's father, then a child, by way of a surgical procedure, and from then on the Aaps—as he called them according to the Dutch word meaning ape—had welcomed, respected and loved him.

For nearly 60 years, Van Kock had lived among these creatures in which he recognized certain aptitudes—still rudimentary—akin to that of humanity. He had taken To-Ho under his wing, had looked after him, taught him. Having recognized in the Aaps the capacity for language in a primitive state, he had developed it. To-Ho, in turn, had taken on the task of educating the tribe.

But, among the hundred or so mating pairs which made the tribe up, at best only a third had truly gained from his teachings. Further, their numbers decreased from year to year as a result of a mysterious form of consumption which Van Kock had tried, in vain, to fight, Only To-Ho and five of his fellows had truly managed to draw themselves up, little by little, to the dignity of man.

Among the others, there was a continuous alternation between progress and decadence. Their anthropoid instincts were the strongest, but, oddly enough, these mixed with human vices blossomed into something evil and perverse. Thus, the few tools which Van Kock had managed to teach them how to make and use, had become weapons in their brutal and deadly battles. The rudimentary clothing which they had to be taught how to make had become an excuse for petty jealousies and ridiculous ornamentation.

The Aapas in particular—the females—had understood with a surprising rapidity what such or such finery—seed necklaces, flowered head-dresses, screens of twigs—could add to what they considered—the poor she-apes—to be their beauty. To the pure and simple instinct of the distinction between Aaps of different types, had come to be juxtaposed preferences born from vanity, coquetry and jealousy. And, by a stunning prescience of human stupidity, these primitive creatures had come to elect gold as a sign of superiority, of power and of love!

Gold! Which could be found in its native state in the torrents! Which sometimes emerged from the outcrops and valleys! Which sparkled in crushed minerals!

Kock was the first to cry out: "Gold is the enemy!"

And To-Ho had understood, especially the day when the prospectors, venturing to the confines of this wilderness, had killed some of the Aaps to take possession of their hidden stashes, had killed his poor little son, who had committed no other crime than being unable to answer those who wished to compel him to reveal the location of the gold deposits! How much this concept of the perversity of gold had grown when To-Ho had once ventured among men and had seen for himself that gold conferred upon its owners an all-powerful evil!

In this thick-lobed brain, with its ill-defined convolutions, ideas were vaguely manifest, ponderous, like those which arise in a drowsy state, in a half-light. Kock had shown him gold as the creator of discord and murder, and this had led him to a concept whose simplicity had struck him: One must destroy gold, everywhere and always!

How? This was Kock's secret, and he had waited many years to confer it to To-Ho, so much had he feared that the anthropoid, in one of those excesses of rage under which his bestial instincts returned to the surface—but were becoming, it is true, more and more infrequent—did not use the power of which he, Kock, was the wise protector—to cause some horrific catastrophe.

What was Kock's discovery? We have mentioned that, for a long time, beginning with the hypothesis of the unity of matter, he had studied the procedures through which the alchemists strove to transform metals—lead and mercury—into gold. Kock had reasoned that perhaps the regressive process was easier, that is the breaking down of gold—no longer considered a simple substance—into its materials of origin. Gold, he was convinced, was a ripened metal; he knew that, in the mines of Mexico, native workers frequent discard gold-bearing minerals, stating that "This gold is not ripe," believing that the mineral, to reach a full state of *goldness* required further incubation under the influence of both subterranean and solar heat.

Hence the conclusion that gold, ripened, could conversely rot like a fruit, to break down and no longer be like unto itself, no more so than the peach or cherry, or any organic matter, which, through decomposition, loses it texture and shape. To destroy gold, such that its very substance decomposed, such was the challenge Van Kock had set for himself. For years, he had conducted endless experiments. Under the preconceived notion that gold must decompose at temperatures exceeding those under which it had been formed, he had tried to apply a heat greater than that of the Sun. He had burned down entire forests to create such a monstrously incandescent furnace, but had failed. The gold melted, but returned as an imperishable ingot.

One day, in the laboratory which he himself had built, and which was a temple-like site of frightened veneration to the Aaps—he was subjecting some minerals he had found in the mountains to a process of analysis. The decomposition had occurred; Kock had ascertained that the dissociated elements were known to him, and after a superficial examination, he had left, closing the door to his hut behind him.

He had returned, alone, at night, and had suddenly stopped short, dumbfounded. Through the window which he had carved out of a block of mica, he perceived a strangely glittering soft white glow. What was happening in there? He was quite sure that he had not lit the resin lamp which normally illuminated the premises, and besides, what a difference between the lamp's fuliginous yellow light and this one of star-like clarity!

He entered. The seat of this glow was in the crucible: with a feverish haste, he observed, studied, in the bottom of the matrass a mass—metallic, mineral—lay, and from this mass emanated a certain light and a certain warmth. A thundering revelation! Matter was its own source of power and motion! With what passion did he return to his study, what dangers did he confront! As he extracted more of the mysterious metal from the large deposit of minerals at the bottom of the valley, he observed some of its stunning and rather terrifying effects.

The new metal, having in itself the power to produce light and heat, that is to say emitting many million vibrations per second, was a terrible agent of disintegration. The more Van Kock purified it, obtained it in its native form, the more the power which emanated from it frightened him: a hundredth of a milligram dashed against the hardest stone was enough to pulverize it. At its contact, the most refractory of metals—gold—was in some manner volatilized.

With a kilo of this material, Van Kock could have blown up the planet.

He varied his experiments, verified them, expanded them, and realized, with a certain terrified pride, that he was the master of life on Earth, that he could, if he so wished, annihilate it in one fell stroke...What was the point? Why not let men live their lives, evolve slowly towards progress? Van Kock was too high-minded to think of avenging himself of them, of their stupidity!

He thought of returning to the world, armed with this formidable power. He told himself that, thanks to it, industry would take a new leap forward, that the world would take on a new face, that mountains would subside and allow the peoples of the world to better mix and extend a hand to one another! For a moment, this dream of humanity—through the power of science—haunted him and nearly drove him mad. He regained his self-control: if man had a right to the title of superior race, what joy would it have been to place in their hands such a tool for progress, to solve all mechanical problems, to revamp the transport industry, and in a word, to tame the Earth, and struggle on equal footing against the blind forces of Nature.

But Van Kock remembered that men would first and foremost use this power to destroy, enslave and pillage; unleash yet more awful wars, and, in an appalling conflict of ambitions, the entire world would collapse! He resigned himself to keeping his wonderful and dangerous secret, but, at least, he could use it to protect his friends, those he had elected to call brothers, To-Ho and his friends.

Thanks to the substance he had named *phobium*, so baptized in honor of the Sun, he could repel the invasion of the gold- seekers, showing them by the destruction of the lodes the inanity of their attempts. With the most thorough precautions, he had initiated To-Ho to the handling of the terrible compound. He had entrusted him with a wand bearing at its tip a capsule containing a tiny bit of phobium, with which gold needed only be touched for it to break down and be transformed into a black muck in which the most thorough chemical analysis would have found no vestige of the precious metal. In this manner, he had frequently destroyed piles of nuggets gathered and stored by the Aaps themselves in their vague longings for luxury and riches. So, too, had he transformed the beginning of mines into veritable cesspools before which even the boldest prospectors had retreated.

Lastly, in a spirit of precaution, Van Kock had not revealed to To-Ho how the mysterious material was made, nor the more devastating effects one could obtain with it.

These explanations given—somewhat lengthy, but indispensable to one's understanding of this story—let us return to our two characters, the man and the pithecanthrope, who, as we have stated, were headed for a location in the valley where shouting and laughing could be heard.

Having made it through a narrow defile, formed by two steep basalt outcroppings, as if they had been split by a great sword, they suddenly found themselves in a sort of small cirque, closed off on all sides by irregular rock faces, almost completely hidden by green tufts.

An exclamation of surprise and anger escaped them. The scene which presented itself to their eyes was at the same time so strange and so burlesque that the cause of their stupefaction was self evident. On a mound in the middle of the cirque, a female Aap was prone, half stretched out on a pile of branches: she bore on her brow a kind of diadem of scarlet red flowers and about her neck, her shoulders, her arms, her legs, was twisted, snake-like, a braid of lianas within which gold nuggets were ensconced.

About her, other females had arranged themselves, with a singular sense of staging and the theatrical, on the sloping surfaces of the mound. There, in studied poses— more bizarre than gracious, and grotesque by the ugliness of the attendants—were the worshippers, or rather the priestesses, of the chosen idol. It was like a rudimentary form of feminine coquetry, something brutal, savagely impassioned with color and light. Where had they found the pieces of rock crystal, the bright many hued stones?

Clumsier still, more tasteless than she who, in the middle of them, stood as a kind of queen or goddess, they had wrapped themselves up, ensheathed in gemstones, nuggets, lianas and flowers, and through this weave appeared, in its perfect ugliness, their black skin, its hair standing up in tufts.

They simpered, laughed, growled, rolled their eyes so that only the white sclera appeared, while with their arms and legs they went through a range of inharmonious gestures. But this was nothing before the incredible and fantastic spectacle offered by the older Aaps. These truly looked like a troop of insane devils. Upright, gesticulating, howling, bounding about, somersaulting, they whirled in a Sabbath ring around the goddess' pedestal. Others, no less mad, no less unbalanced, struck with might and main on pieces of wood, the clapping of which, in its insufferable dissonances, managed to create a horrible cacophony.

Oddly enough, these primitive creatures understood the concept of differing sounds. For his musical rendition, each had chosen a piece of wood and a stone, which, struck together, gave a note unlike that of the others. Tones and notes were tangled into an inextricable muddle, made all the more tiresome by the fact that the resonances were loud, dull and with no holding of the note. But what gave this orchestra a more diabolical character, was that it complemented itself with vocal accompaniment—and what voices! Nothing but shrieks, drawn from the throat, from the chest, at times similar to the gurgling of liquids in a narrow conduit, at times loud, raucous, emitted from the depths of the rib-cage.

It seemed that each of these creatures only had a few specific vociferations in its repertoire, which it repeated in an invariable sequence, with greater or lesser gusto, according to the rhythm. This was actually the profound difference which existed between these vocal manifestations and those of wild animals, birds excepted, of course. While the roar of the lion, the tiger, the hissing of the serpent, the trumpeting of the elephant, the neighing of the horse, or the braying of the donkey always sound the same for a given individual, proving that they are not masters of their voices and only utter their cry in a reflexive act, the Aaps on the contrary seemed to gauge the range, length and frequency of their cries.

As they were just then at the peak of their exaltation, these cries, following, on average, a six-part scale, but of which the irregularities were innumerable—a discordant, croaking, bellowing musical Babel—was insufferable to listen to. Laughs arose like sudden yelps, their bodies engaged in convulsive movements, and this fury was shared by the male, female and infant Aaps who danced about in an epileptic whirlwind.

Van Kock had immediately understood: with the exception of a group of six to eight Aaps, who had taken refuge in a rocky corner, and, in a near panic, watched wide-eyed this demonic scene, these creatures were all drunk. Drunk? How? Certainly To-Ho knew that some had discovered, by breaking up and crushing berries easily found in the rich vegetation, a way to make up a liquor which they then allowed to ferment. This produced a state of intoxication, or rather of poisoning, the effects of which Van Kock had often had to deal with. However, until now, this had only engendered a passing agitation amongst them, free of any convulsive symptoms.

Never had the To-Ho seen his brothers in such a state of outrageous degradation. They seemed oblivious to all but their chants and dances. To-Ho ran to those who had remained calm and questioned them. He had trouble understanding their answers, especially since the rudimentary language they used among themselves contained too few vocables to express ideas which were perhaps new. Van Kock had drawn near, and having listened, his greater intellect had soon led him to a solution to the mystery.

"Come," he said to To-Ho in the Dutch they had convened upon, "and let our six friends follow us courageously."

He pushed forward resolutely through the groups of convulsives, bumping into them and pushing them aside. They staggered, lurched about, and fell. While the weakest among them could have seized the doctor in its huge hands and crushed him to a pulp, they did not interfere, besotted and stupefied as they were.

TO-HO, LE TUEUR D'OR
Van Kock se lança résolument à travers les groupes des convulsionnaires. (P. 328, col. 1.)

He pushed forward resolutely through the groups of convulsives.

To-Ho had obeyed Van Kock's order, and thus the two had reached, followed by the sober Aaps, the base of the mound upon which the females were perched, and as they sought to move them aside, the simian shrews huddled together, their nails darting forward, forming something resembling a phalanx of old-time spear- bearers.

Van Kock was slashed full in the face, one held on to To-Ho, trying to scratch out his eyes, while the others, furious, ground their teeth, raking with their claws those they could reach, biting and grimacing in a forbidding manner. However, in a vigorous push forward, To-Ho and his followers managed to make their way through, and suddenly Van Kock cried out. Their support, the soft cushions upon which the she-apes—since for the moment they did not deserve to be designated otherwise—lay prostrate in their poetic poses, were four casks, three of which were breached and from which trickled what was left of a liquor which Van Kock, the good Dutchman, recognized at first smell as a choice gin.

The barrels had been breached at random, the brutes had thrown themselves flat on their bellies to drink, even licking the moistened soil. They were soon so drunk that they had not even noticed that the last barrel was still untouched. How could have the barrels gotten there? From where had the Aaps brought them?

"Are men then that close to us?" said Van Kock. "Ah! These wretches will be unknowing traitors and bring ruin to their poor tribe."

To-Ho, as well, had understood what had caused this great drunkenness: all had drunk themselves mad, females and males alike. The former had hastened to dig up gold nuggets which they had buried to subtract them from Van Kock's searches. To-Ho did not hesitate, he went straight to the remaining barrel, and raising it with his two arms extended, he leaned it on his shoulder; then, roaring out in an authoritative tone to make way for him, he began to walk. His aim was to toss it into one of the mountain's crevasses. Those which had accompanied him had grouped themselves around him.

Meanwhile, in the blink of an eye, Van Kock, drawing from his clothing a phobium-bearing wand, had touched the gold nuggets scattered about the ground. There was a sort of crackling sound and the metal burst apart, dissolving into muck. Remarkably, each small piece of spatter seemed to be imbued with the same properties as phobium, and the gold seem to break down through some sort of process of contagion.

The females were the first to take notice of the work to which Van Kock was applying himself, and, angered, ran to defend their treasures, throwing themselves to ground, picking up great handfuls of muck, wailing before this transformation, trying to save the non-gangrenous nuggets. But the last pieces of gold, which had so far remained intact, burst apart between their fingers. They cried out, put their hands to their head, to their shoulders, as if to preserve the rudimentary jewelry which they had crafted, and these, barely touched, snapped in two, collapsed, crumbled into a viscous brown powder.

At the sight of their treasure reduced to nothing, the females entered a state of indescribable fury, giving themselves up to horrific contortions of terror. Their rage now unbound, they charged towards Van Kock to tear him apart. Backing away, fighting them back as best he could, he rediscovered a vigor which belied his age. However the exasperation of these shaggy furies increased their strength ten-fold.

"To-Ho! To-Ho!" cried out the Dutchman, "Help me! Help me!"

But To-Ho, for his part, was fighting the Aaps, who irritated to see the barrel of gin taken away, had thrown themselves in front of him to block his passage. He spoke to them, but in vain. Helped by his fellows, who, being sober, had remained loyal to him, he tried in vain to fray a passage. Every minute the danger grew greater.

These primitive creatures—usually so docile, indolent and indifferent—were maddened by this noxious drink. How had they gotten their hands on it?

They were prospectors, bolder than the rest, who had come near the Aaps' retreat and had pitched, in this wild gorge, a camp from which they thought to explore the country. The Aaps had come upon them by surprise and would have been content to put them to flight, had not the Europeans, terrified by these fantastic apparitions, defended themselves with gun-fire. Two Aaps had fallen, stuck down by bullets. Then, the others, angered and made that much more courageous given their ignorance of the danger, had charged their adversaries, surrounded them and proceeded to massacre them to the last.

Then, rediscovering the atavistic instincts of simian brutes, they had pillaged the tents, broken the weapons, the tools, torn the fabrics and clothes, until the moment when they came upon the barrels of liquor and chanced to discover what was in them. One can guess the rest; how, loading these small casks on their shoulders, they had brought them back to their lair. Already hypocrites, and knowing through some singular intuition that To-Ho was not to be informed of their adventures, they had come to hide out in this remote part of the valley, and the orgy had begun. Males and females had gorged themselves on the burning gin, the flavor of which was unknown to them, and now, they were quickly regressing to the level of the lowest apes.

The only humanity which remained in them was their perverse instinct for instant gratification. Under the influence of drunkenness, their basest animal instincts were revealed, and, in a few hours, all the work towards progress attempted and half- achieved by Van Kock and To-Ho, was destroyed. The Aaps were now no more than simians regressed to an intimacy with a state of mindless and fierce bestiality.

To-Ho had heard his friend's call for help, the man whom he considered his father, he whom had passed on some of his humanity to him, and whom, in the dimness of his still dormant consciousness, had brought on the dawning of progress. He leapt to a boulder and, from there, saw that Van Kock about to succumb to his frantic attackers.

So, using the barrel he was carrying as a big club, he ploughed through the Aaps, whom, from a sense of fraternity which had developed little by little in his consciousness, he had until then tried to spare. However, he now sensed a greater duty: saving his benefactor.

His leap was so powerful that he immediately reached him, and, with a few well placed clouts, he dispersed the females, who ran way towards the Aaps, crying out discordantly. These, still overexcited by the much-deserved treatment their mates had just received, began to break off slabs of rock and stone the two friends. The apes were strong, and, as the strength they exerted was increased two-fold by their fevered state, they were able to detach huge blocks of stone. They got together, ten of them, to hoist them uphill, and from there rolled them down onto their adversaries, whom on several occasions had almost been crushed.

To-Ho had placed himself in front of Van Kock and skillfully managed to deflect the blows, but it was clear that this could not go on for long. The place where this scene was unfolding was a sort of cirque, enclosed on all sides by steep rocky pitches which could not be climbed. The only way out: the cleft through which To-Ho and Van Kock had entered. This was now occupied by the Aaps, raging mad and determined to kill To-Ho, the one who they considered to be their implacable enemy, the one who had torn the barrel from their clutches, and who had now broken it by hurling it to the ground.

The Aaps saw this, the stream of the beverage spreading over the soil that drank it up, absorbed it. They howled out furiously in rage and disappointment. The stones rained down thicker and faster on the two friends, until, suddenly, one of the Aaps had a devilish idea. The entire cirque was covered in tall and very dry grasses. The attack suddenly stopped. Was this a lull? Had exhaustion overcome their fury? Was peace imminent? Such delusions could not hold, for if To-Ho and Van Kock took a single step towards the gorge, the stoning immediately started afresh, more violent and more dangerous.

Already To-Ho had been struck in the head, drawing blood. Van Kock had been knocked over and had been unable to rise without a great effort.

"Whatever are they doing?" muttered the Dutchman in his comrade's ear. "See that small group which hides behind the attackers and around which the females busy themselves, with gestures of curiosity and admiration... my sight is weakened, I can't make it out."

To-Ho had gone up on the mound, watching. Suddenly, he cried out in surprise, in terror:

"*Vou! Vou!*" he cried out with all his breath. This word, which was the basis of the Dutch word *voor*, meant fire!

Van Kock understood and cried out in turn:

"We are lost! And I'm the one who taught them this!"

This being the way to make fire by with a quickly rotated hand drill in a dry hearth board. Suddenly, reality showed them that they had indeed guessed correctly: the Aaps had managed to light a clump of dry grass, and, with savage cries, had just fired the brush in the cirque.

There was a series of tiny crackles, followed by small detonations at an increasing frequency, and, suddenly, a flame shot up, brilliant, conquering, propagating itself at an amazingly rate, running, in a circle at first, along the rocks, encircling the two friends in a ring of fire. To-Ho and Van Kock were chilled by what they saw. Here was death, painful and horrific!

Escape? It was impossible! The Aaps, whose demonic instincts had not deceived them—closed off the gorge, ready to escape when the sinister work was accomplished. They hailed their craven victory with fierce roars. The females excited them, shook their fists at the two doomed to die and spat in their direction.

The fire was accomplishing its work, a quiet rumble came from the brush. At times, it seemed the flames had died out, but the smoke which came out above the canopy of twigs were proof that it continued its sly advance, and all of sudden horizontal flames would rocket through the vegetation, tracing out the extent of the fire.

A flame shot up, encircling the two friends in a ring of fire.

Little by little, the area which remained unscathed shrank. To-Ho and Van Kock ran from the scourge that pursued and hemmed them in. To-Ho had tried ten times to climb the rocks, but had fallen back. Van Kock, having concluded that any attempt was futile, remained calm, his head bent against his chest, pensive as if absorbed in an internal meditation. There was a new burst of fire, the entire rear of the cirque was burning, and the victims were pushed back towards the gorge where the Aaps waited for them, waited to push them back into the furnace.

The six apes which had refused, since these events had begun, to take up the cause of their fellows, broke away with their mates from the group of assailants and ran towards To-Ho. They came to die with him. They were barely in time to accomplish their sacrifice, as now, between the edge of the fire and the entrance to the gorge there remained barely ten meters, somewhat clearer and where the fire could not take hold.

This afforded them a few minutes of respite, the heat gradually becoming intolerable in this restricted area, where standing was no longer possible. Nonetheless, To-Ho wished to make a final attempt. The poor wretch, who had so often sacrificed himself for the sake of his fellows, who had dreamed of raising them little by little to a level above mere animality, who, as the last survivor of a race whose origin was lost in the mists of time, had conceived of a life of greater self-perception, of a wider-ranging intelligence, intimations of which had made their way to the very core of his being, now saw his work lost.

He saw the torture of Van Kock whose goodness and patience had open new, as yet unknown, moral horizons to him; of his faithful friends, less evolved than he, who had nonetheless proven, by their admirable sacrifice, that they were worthy of rising higher on the ladder of life. He also thought of his mate, of the child of men which he had wanted to save and which these brutes stupidly held in a paroxysm of vengeance. He spoke, adjured his fellows, his friends, his brothers to give up their barbaric designs. He begged them to allow them to pass.

In so doing, he used the apes' language, made up of inflexions and growls. In his despair, the language which Van Kock had managed to decipher, notwithstanding its incomplete and rudimentary expressions, revealed a painful and almost sublime nobility of spirit. He was met with boos, shouts, bitter and worsening discord. He was doomed, and with him Van Kock and his friends.

Turning towards the Dutchman, he whispered: "My poor Waa!"

But Van Kock, shuddering as one waking from a deep sleep, looked around him. Death—and what a death!—was only a matter of minutes, perhaps seconds away.

"Upon my word! It's too damn bad!" he cried out in turn. "Never have I killed anyone, but since it must be done..."

He brandished the wand of phobium, which he had not parted with. It was equipped within with a skillfully assembled spring which could throw the terrible substance over a fairly long distance. He hesitated another instant; at that very moment, To-Ho was struck full in the chest by a stone, whose impact bent him over, one could expect no mercy.

Van Kock brandished his weapon and released the spring. The piece of phobium struck glancingly one face of the gorge and ricocheted across to the other side. Instantly, the entire mass was cleared away, collapsed, pulverized, burying in a black muck the Aaps who had not even conceived of the danger. At the same time, on either side, thanks to the collapse, paths of escape were opened.

"Forward!" cried Van Kock.

The small group sprang forward and, at the very instant they reached the miraculous exit, the entire cirque fell prey to the fire—but they were saved.

To-Ho and Van Kock ran, breathless to the top of the hill. Waa was beside George; he had neither seen nor heard anything, the human child played with the she-ape, who was all smiles.

Chapter IV

The catastrophe in the gorge had had terrible consequences. The population of Aapland was suddenly reduced to twenty-odd families, and among those which
had witnessed the cataclysm, terror had brought on a sort
of nervous breakdown which was translated in a regres-
sion to an animal state.

To-Ho himself had felt the backlash of this terrible
jolt. Certain he did not blame Van Kock for his liberat-
ing act, to which he owed his life and that of his friends,
but in spite of himself, the old Dutchman now inspired
him with a feeling of dread which he could not shake. It
was also that Van Kock had never revealed to him the
awesome destructive potential of phobium, whose power
he believed to be limited to the destruction of gold. In
this roughshod brain, wherein the cerebral lobes operated in a sort of torpor, ideas, slowly developed, only af-
firmed themselves after a long incubation, as if they
must first, through patient work, be freed of their gan-
gue.

Van Kock now appeared to him as a creature gifted
with staggering powers, belonging to the strange frightening race, which he had only glimpsed through a fog
of blood. The brave Dutchman, who, when all was said
and done, had only been led to carry out his work of destruction in order to snatch him from death, thinking
more of the ape and his friends that of himself, had tried,
but in vain, to bring him back to a more sound understanding of things.

To-Ho still showed him the same affection, but Van
Kock noticed that, when the primitive creature con-

versed with him, an unexplained anxiousness made his tawny hair stand up on end. However, the child brought them together. George finally recovered from his great fatigue and fears, and quickly got used to the strange world in which he lived. Besides, the kind-hearted Waa was subject to his every whim, and he quickly abused of this tireless complacency with the unconscious despotism of spoiled children.

To-Ho and his mate, as well as the other Aaps, struck George as being inferior creatures, animals over which his humanity conferred him a limitless authority. He felt in no way drawn to the increasingly ugly and now almost centenarian Van Kock. Certainly the latter's continuous association with the apes had impressed upon his physiognomy and his gait a truly simian character. Thus do spouses, though a long life together, come to resemble each other physically.

His bristly hair and beard, his face crisscrossed with a thousand creases, Van Kock was truly uglier than a monkey, and the goodwill of his intelligent gaze did not compensate, in the eyes of the young man, the grotesque strangeness of his exterior.

Besides, in his estimation, Van Kock had another fault. George's education was rather rudimentary: it was not around Kota-Rajia that he would have acquired much learning. The old Dutchman had taken on the task of teaching him the elements of science, especial chemistry and the natural sciences. To-Ho, his paternal instincts regained, knew not how to refuse the young man—perhaps the "child" might be a better term—whose preference was to go on long excursions in the mountains and through the forests.

Besides, To-Ho was a gymnastics professor of a caliber one would have had great difficulty in finding: foot races and jumping were games to him, and George had quickly become a fine student. A way of communicating had established itself between them, aided by an expressive pantomime. Naturally the number of concepts which To-Ho could make use of was limited, but in these solitudes no consideration necessitated anything more. George had fun, laughed, ran about, amused himself playing all sorts of tricks, teasing the good-hearted ape, whose naivety was a never-ending source of joy to him.

Very proud of his humanity, having barely understood what Van Kock had told him of the intermediate position of To-Ho in the ladder of life, he often tried to amaze him by telling him of human civilization, of the luxuries of cities, of the extent of industry. Especially, given his initial education and his youth, he glorified war and tried to make To-Ho understand the wonders of battle and of military history.

To-Ho listened; he indeed remembered having seen at Kota-Rajia men who threw themselves upon other men, while the air around him exploded in frightful detonations; the creatures dropped in pools of blood—all this had he seen. He also remembered the man with the impassive face, who, covered in gold and gems, had struck and tortured him for hours. As the ape seemed to have no interest in stories of war and carnage, he appeared to be rather silly to the child of men.

Besides, To-Ho's imagination was incapable of conjuring up the grandiose events which George attempted to describe, so, when George had been speaking and gesticulation for awhile, the ape would pick a nice ripe fruit, fragrant and colorful, hand it to him with a hearty laugh and say:

"This, good!" he stated simply.

159

Also, to the description of the riches and splendors of Europe, which George obligingly spread out before him, To-Ho, in whose understanding these concepts remained vague and obscure, answered by merely indicating in a sweeping gesture the deep, luminous sky, the huge trees, full of life, the blue-shaded mountains, as well as the sun's radiant disk bursting forth from the boundless firmament.

"Good ape," George said to him while pulling his ears, "you'll never amount to anything."

The ape laughed, thankful for this somewhat scornful intimacy, but which did constitute a caress. Besides, life was so easy, the food so tasty and abundant, that George would sometimes forget his past. Quite good with his hands, he spent his time plaiting lianas and had built himself his own furniture. The good Waa was thrilled.

In a recess amongst the rocks George had created a genuine bedroom, completely carpeted in matting, with rudimentary bamboo furniture. It was one of Waa's little pleasures to come in the morning and watch him wake in his bed, which had indeed turned out well, and was padded with ferns, which the good Aap chose amongst the softest and downiest.

To-Ho—and this brought down constant ridicule upon him—preferred sleeping in a tree, between the highest branches. Waa, more of a sybarite, curled up in the huge leaves of the Taolak, which she pulled over her like covers. Van Kock, himself, slept on the ground, in front of the door of his laboratory. No one crossed its threshold, and besides, George showed no interest in trying to discover its secrets, having a healthy dose of superstitious fear.

However, the young man's curiosity had been awakened on several occasions. How was it that from old Van Kock's cabin there came smoke, when neither To-Ho nor his friends had ever made fire since the events in the cirque, which had brought on the catastrophe we are acquainted with. He had questioned To-Ho, who did not care to give him a clear answer. Fire had hurt him too deeply; the price imposed by his remorse too great for him to renew the terrible experiment. Only Van Kock was allowed to light one, and then again, only in his cabin, with the doors closed.

George, to whom no one had told what had happened, was surprised and irritated to not have fire at his disposal, especially since a rather unique idea had come to him. Having found clumps of dry grass which resembled tobacco and gave off a strong and aromatic smell, an irresistible urge had come over him. He wanted to smoke.

To-Ho would not give him the time of day and obstinately refused to show him how to light the wood. George, had instinctively tried rubbing sticks together, but this requires a vigor and perseverance which were not his. He discovered a type of mushroom, whose flesh reminded him of tinder, which he had seen his father use to light his pipe. Mysteriously, he went to work, searching for the hardest flint. When To-Ho had saved him, he had had in his pocket a small children's knife, which he has since tossed away haphazardly. He found it again, and thus improvised a lighter with which he struck the stones, and finally, one day, he managed to strike sparks which lit the dried lamellae of the agaric.

To-Ho was not nearby, and, as he was looking for his young friend, going from branch to branch so as to see him from a greater distance, he found him all of a sudden, very solemnly puffing spirals of smoke into the air. The ape was terribly afraid. The child must be sick. What could this unknown phenomenon be? A blaze in one's stomach? To-Ho leapt towards the child and in an instinctive movement, tore from his lips the rather primitive cigar, made of dry leaves.

Annoyed, George jumped on him, hitting him, trying—furious as he was—to hurt him, to avenge himself. To-Ho did not letting it bother him, grabbed him around the waist, put him under his arm—he was then 15 and was well developed—and took him to Van Kock to whom he explained his alarm.

The old Dutchman, displeased with the boy's carefree attitude and his indifference to science, had little by little lost interest in him, continuing alone the studies he had undertaken. When To-Ho had put George back on his feet and in his primitive language had described the phenomenon which he had witness, Van Kock was at first surprised. He questioned the young man, whose resistance had been broken by the ape and who no longer thought of putting up a fight. The boy told of his adventures and showed the knife which had served as a striker.

Van Kock knotted his brow. Such a discovery could have fatal consequences for the already weakened Aaps tribe; plants chosen at random might contain poisonous principles, intoxication might follow and lead to another catastrophe. He confiscated the knife. Furious, George screamed, stormed about, threatened. Van Kock remained unmoved and went back to his cabin. The young man in fit of anger threw himself against the door which he wish to bust down. To-Ho was forced to tie him up, and he only calmed down after quite awhile.

But from then on, something had died between him and To-Ho. In vain was the latter's kindness greater than ever, seeking to vary the distractions, agreeing to satisfy all his whims. George felt himself more and more becoming a man; he bluntly spurned the advances of the one he called a brute under his breath. Another circumstance, feeding this antipathy coupled with ingratitude, brought on a crisis.

During his peregrinations, which at times led him far from the hearth, and worried To-Ho, George had found a few gold nuggets in a dry creek bed. As young as he had been torn from life among men, he already had in his mind, in his very blood—one might say—the respect, love, and passion of the precious metal. He had avidly collected the nuggets, and, full of pride, had returned to show them to the ape.

To-Ho lacked intellectual initiative, thought and acted mechanically, through a sort of reflexive action. When George, excited, dropped the glittering material before him, the ape instantly took up the wand which Van Kock had entrusted to him and touched the gold, which crumbled, disaggregated and turned into muck. It was too much! George was livid, and again Van Kock was called. This time the centenarian spoke.

"Child," he said, "you understand nothing of what goes on here; you human instincts are preventing you from enjoying the comforts amongst which you live. I have tried to explain to you that these primitive creatures have the great good fortune of not being subject to our worst passions. They ignore ambition, jealousy, and war. Amid Nature, in whose effluvia they bask, they are happy to live and ask for nothing more: this is why I admire them and have remained among them. You consider them to be mere brutes, but you are wrong, as having escaped from animality, they have lost their ferocious brutality, but not yet having attained humanity, have not yet acquired the perversities you yourself know of, since it is to human cruelty to which you owe the death of those you loved and who loved you.

"Perhaps you are surprised that I have not revealed to them a number of civilization's secrets, which, according to you, would have improved their lot. Yes, in the past, I had dreamed of raising them up little by little—I called it 'raising' in those days—to the level of more evolved humans. I taught them the basics of a language, they used it to threaten and insult each other; I taught them to make fire with two pieces of wood, and they tried to burn me like a heretic; I taught the females to clothe themselves in lianas and leaves, and their damned coquetry almost led to violence and murder.

"Finally, the gold they found on the surface of the ground seduced them, and already they had begun to amass treasures, from whence would have emerged, in the short term, civil war and the enslavement of the poor by the rich. This is why, son, I have taught the wisest among them how to destroy gold, as the most dangerous enemy they could ever meet! Because there is much I haven't told you: men, in their lust for wealth, in their ever-present greed, are not without knowing that in this virgin country, under a blinding Sun—the planet's life-giver—gold, the most perfect metal of all is born, grows and matures more quickly than anywhere else. The stillness even, the silence which reigns in these fortunate regions allows Nature free reign to better perfect her mysterious work.

"In these solitudes, gold is abundant; men sense this, know it, and already 20 expeditions have been prepared, targeted at these as yet inaccessible plateaux, but which, tomorrow, human industry will deliver to the miners' pick. And if this were to occur, if the human stampede invaded this peaceful and happy Eden, the first victims would be these good and loving creatures, which are the link between the overly ferocious animal kingdom and the overly intelligent human one.

"I have already tried to explain this to you, but you refused to listen. You are a man and, unlike me ,you have been unable to come to the scientific serenity, which makes goodwill and justice supreme. Yes, I made To-Ho a gold-destroyer, so that he would not, one day, think of becoming a destroyer of men. He defends himself, and his tribe, by destroying that which draws, pushes and makes men mad. He fights the invasion which would be followed by the advent of alcohol and all the madness it brings—of this I have had ample evidence—strife in all its forms, despotism, the exploitation of the weak, and finally death.

"These creatures, which you despise, do not know about fighting for their lives, that which makes the lands of men a field of carnage; they are good because they have in profusion what they require to subsist, and they do not create themselves any artificial needs. They love one another, help each other, save one another from harm because they know of no other animals but the wild beasts of the forests or the blind forces of Nature. I have tried everything to maintain this happy state for them... Child of man, have you understood?"

At first, George had silently protested against these injunctions which, altogether, ran counter to his immediate whims, but, in reality, he was neither unintelligent nor ill-natured, and, as the old man spoke, his features relaxed. Little by little, the grandeur and simplicity of these ideas reached him, were instilled in him; he understood the great distance which separated the mild and patient behavior of these primitive creatures from the fury and ferocity he had seen in men, their calls for death, their rush to attack the weak.

To-Ho had also listened, with an almost painful concentration, if the contraction of his features and the knitting of his brow were any indication. It was clear that he barely understood Van Kock's speech; but every fiber of his brain, all the energy of his obscure intellect resembled the strings of an instrument which vibrate to the point of snapping. All he knew was that there were creatures, somewhat similar to him, violent and cruel, and drawn by gold: yes, he was knowingly a gold-destroyer, an enemy to his enemies.

And, watching George, he wondered if these many words, which he barely understood, would manage to convince this child of man, which he loved with all his primitive instincts, and who was not and could never be an enemy.

"Did you understand me? repeated Van Kock. "I hope so. Now listen to this: in truth, you are free. If you so wish, I will take you back, myself among men. No one has the right to hold you prisoner against your will... Yes I will lead you to the farthest borders of Aapland, and will teach you how to reach your fellows...but will you at least promise me to not betray us?"

"Me!" cried out the young man. "Do you really think me capable of such a thing?"

"You are a man, I tell you, and once among men, recaptured by the environment's perversity, perhaps you will remember that vast wealth which resides in these mountains; you will talk; expeditions will be organized, and you will serve as their guide... I tell you, we will defend ourselves with desperation. Science, thanks to my 60 years of study, has delivered fearful secrets unto me; if we must, we will sustain a siege; it will cost them more dearly than the most sinister episodes of human wars. This is what you can do with freedom, head for men and talk; otherwise, remain among us, work, ask the sphinx which is Nature the answer to the most troubling questions... Live in the worthy pleasure of intellectual labor, in the wonderful well-being which a complacent Nature gives you. Choose!"

In a burst of juvenile enthusiasm, George extended his hands to Van Kock and exclaimed: "I'm staying!"

Chapter V

The years went by. A complete transformation had occurred in George Villiers' character.

His childhood indifference had made room for a passion for learning. Still, for some time, Van Kock had showed himself to be suspicious, but, little by little, he came to value one who asked only to be his student. But there was one point upon which, unknowingly, the teacher and student were not wholly in agreement: for Van Kock, a fugitive from human society, any theories were limited in their application to the very small group within which he lived.

Wrapped up in his speculations, he dreamed of creating from this stock of anthropoids, a new race, one which, having slowly evolved towards complete understanding, would take over the Earth. Then, they would establish a utopian society based upon equality and justice for all. These new men, the direct offsprings of Nature, would ignore social dissensions and rivalries; none would dominate, none would seek to amass wealth, and a universal solidarity would reign, in its fullest and purest form.

George, in listening to him, had grasped all the grandeur, all the beauty of these theories, whose implementation, Van Kock said, would be facilitated by the use of the substance he had discovered, and whose power would defy all resistance.

"Meaning that," the young man objected, "to breathe life into your plan, one would first have to destroy the human race, destroy all the advancements of its civilization?"

"Why not?" replied the elderly utopian. "Will our Aaps not soon repopulate the Earth? And if they do not build monuments, at least, in their clusters of huts and fields, none will face starvation again."

"And for this work of benevolence, you would not hesitate, if such power were given to you, to wipe out millions of human beings?"

"For humanity to start afresh? Certainly!"

"Such measures strike me as somewhat radical," objected George, laughing. "But let us move on to another order of business. Have you not noticed, dear master, that this race you count upon to regenerate the world seems to be wasting away day by day? Might one not think that it has been struck down by some sort of epidemic, for every day, death leaves a void among us."

It was true. The Aaps tribe was constantly decreasing. The children no longer thrived and their mothers howled over their corpses. The males grew leaner to the point of acute malnutrition, and one could see them sitting sadly on the cliff edges, staring into space, as if drawn by the abyss; some had even let themselves be taken by this vertigo.

What was happening? To what could one attribute this degeneration? Was it, as Van Kock had whispered in George's ear, the presence of man, which by some mysterious phenomenon, sullied or in some way poisoned the life-giving air and rendered it unsuitable for the survival of these lower creatures?

To-Ho himself was aging: his great torso was somewhat bent, not that his strength had diminished, or that his agility had lessened any, but it seemed that some thought, which he could not formulate, burdened and weighed upon him. George had now become a young man. Waa, judging no doubt that he no longer needed her, now looked upon him with a fearful respect.

Solitude, so beautiful amongst the exuberance of Nature, became silent and burdensome. One day, returning from an excursion through some of the wildest gorges, To-Ho came to a stop before George, who was in quite a happy mood, his youth taking the place of any philosophical considerations.

"Go away!" the ape-man told him abruptly.

"Go away? But why?"

"Because you are a man!"

"I will never leave you."

The Aap thought, then continued:

"Explain to me what a man is!"

George barely knew, for he had lived a savage life for so many years that, beneath his long head of hair, beneath his face framed in a bushy beard, he had almost taken on the appearance of those amongst which he had settled. Only his smooth white skin remained an indelible mark. However, he tried to plead the case for his race to To-Ho.

But all his memories of childhood were linked to scenes of violence and carnage. As a small child, he had, along with his mother and sister, been hunted like a wild beast. Men had wanted to slit his throat and those of all who were dear to him.

"Cruel men!" repeated To-Ho.

"No! Not all. My father was brave and gentle. My mother appears in my memories as an angel of mercy and kindness!"

"You told me that men had killed them."

"It's true!"

Little by little, the fear, the hatred of man, was implanting itself in George's heart. Like Van Kock, like

To-Ho, he came to dread the invasion of Aapland by this dangerous race.

Van Kock never ceased to tell them:

"Destroy the gold, wherever you find it, as it is the bait which attracts them, that calls to them, and in its conquest, they will not shrink before any act of violence, before any crime."

Now To-Ho was obsessed with destroying gold. In that unpolished brain, incapable of overcoming one thought with another, the instinct of self-preservation was all powerful. Continually, he wandered around the domains which Nature had assigned to his fellows, and which each day became too vast for those who would follow. He was on the lookout for gold, divined its presence, smelled it, and, armed with the wand of phobium, he destroyed the least fragment he came across.

George had finally come to interest himself in this hunt, as long as it sometimes led the two of them some great distances from their huts, where he might have the pleasure of devoting himself to sports of stamina and agility. So it was that, one day, as George had ventured on the summit of a peak which overlooked a sharp-sloping plain, he rose up in surprise, and, motioning wildly, called to To-Ho, who, hunched over some soil, sought to recognize the well-known signs of the presence of gold.

The young man's call was so pressing that the ape-man thought he was in imminent danger. In a single prodigious leap, he dropped next to the young man, ready to defend him, and looked in the direction the latter indicated. Silhouettes could be made out, following a barely discernable trail through the thick brush. Men! They were men! They walked in single file, having with them pack horses which carried tents, cooking utensils and tools.

"Ho! Man!" growled To-Ho shaking his giant fist.

George had remained motionless, thoughtful, saddened. There was no mistaking it: these were indeed members of his race who were boldly venturing into these solitudes. To better see them, filled with an anxiety whose origins he could not fathom—consisting of both fear and some strange involuntary attraction—George crept along the crest of the rocky outcrop, peering out, wide-eyed.

The men, for he was not mistaken and these strangers indeed belonged to that dreaded race, seemed undecided, proceeding haphazardly, impeded at every step by the inextricably tangled lianas which presented a nigh impassible barrier to their progress. In spite of himself, George bent over, obeying the irresistible magnetism of men! It was to this family of creatures to which he belonged! Suddenly he was flooded with tender memories.

No, no! Not all men were bad! For in his youth, he had been loved, doted upon, cuddled. Did not his gentle father, who used to hold him in his arms, who walked around with him perched on his shoulders, belong to the race of man? Was not Luisa, his mother, a woman whose kindness was irrefutable, a woman who had sacrificed herself for the happiness and security of her children? Was it not again a child, a little woman, his beloved sister Margaret, towards whom he had assumed the role of protector, and who laughed so heartily at his childish pranks?

He also remembered the cabin on the banks of the great river. There, men and women who differed in some degree from Europeans, but who were also pleasant, had long treated them as if they had been of their own race!

No, not all men were cruel monsters. George, at the sight of the approaching strangers, felt his heart beat faster and tears welling up in his eyes.

Suddenly, while To-Ho, who could not have guessed at these feelings, was flashing his worried and hateful glare over the small troop, George, acting unconsciously, not knowing what drove him, as if seized by an unseen hand which drew him forward, launched himself recklessly down the rocky slope, hanging on to an outcrop, taking hold of a root sticking out between two stones, without regard for the risks of a terrible fall.

To-Ho saw this, and first thought it the result of some accident. He thought the young man had lost his footing, and was going to strike his head on the ground. Good soul that he was, he was moved by the fatherly role he had taken on. In turn, he rushed down, but with greater agility and recklessness, so that he covered the same distance at a rate George could barely aspire to.

But the young man had a big lead. He reached the ground first, and there began to run with all his might in the direction of the strangers. To-Ho, after a huge leap, rolled to a stop on the ground. He remained dazed for an instant, but, quickly, got up again, having recovered his wits, and rushed forward on George's trail.

Why this flight? Why this precipitous escape? To-Ho could not understand. He called out with all he had, with his last ounce of breath, the name he had given George: "Go! Go!"

George began to run with all his might in the direction of the strangers.

But George did not hear him, did not want to hear him. The fascination which consumed him was so irresistible that no power on Earth could stop him. He went on! To-Ho managed to outdistance him, and, throwing himself in his path, wished to grab him by the arm. He reached him, touched him, but feared greatly injuring him! His hold was not sufficiently strong. George, whose emotional over-excitement doubled his strength, freed himself, and ran off even faster.

Thus did they arrive, one chasing the other, on a great stone slab overlooking the path the men were following. Another small effort and George would reach his goal. Already he yelled out, called out. To-Ho leapt beside him. In self-defense, the ape-man resolved, this time, to employ all his strength, even if, for the sake of their safety, he had to brutalize his friend. At this point, both of them appeared as clear silhouettes against the background of the sky.

Other cries could be heard: the men were uttering them, answering George's calls with their own calls for his death. The men had seen them. They stopped, their weapons were aimed, and a rumbling explosion was heard. George, hit, dropped. To-Ho had already heard, back the in the Malay *kraton*, these noises which sounded like thunder.

The men had seen one of the creatures at which they had aimed their weapons fall. They began to run to reach them, to surround them, to finish them off. To-Ho, his arms knotted, tore off a chunk of rock and threw it. There was some swearing and two men remained stretched on the ground... A new salvo rang out. The bullets whistled around To-Ho's ears. He shook himself, gritted his teeth, shook his giant fist at his enemies. Again, they fired on him. A bullet hit him in the shoulder, but could not penetrate his tough hide; however, it made him stagger. Then he became frightened, truly frightened!

Yes, these were indeed men! He could recognize them well now—their ruthlessness and injustice. In the dim understanding that was his, he felt that they themselves had attacked no one and that it was wrong to wish to injure or kill them. And George would fall into the hands of these monsters!

He collected his strength, bent down, took in his arms the young man who lay on the ground, a pool of blood spreading around him, hoisted him on his shoulder in a powerful muscular exertion, and, as he had once carried him as a small child, ran away, straight ahead before him. He knew he was being pursued; he smelled it. There were shouts behind him and the crack of shots rang out in the air. The detonations, multiplied by the cliff-faces, echoed in a sinister manner. His assailants tried to overtake him. One could hear them say:

"Kill! Kill the ape-men!"

But To-Ho did not allow himself to be overtaken. Truly, he seemed to fly through the air. Notwithstanding the burden that weighed down his shoulders, he took prodigious leaps and the distance separating him from his persecutors increased every minute. But the men were armed, which gave them a decided advantage.

"Hey! Ned!" a voice shouted, "you never miss a shot... Take down the ape."

A man climbed up on one of the stone outcroppings, shouldered, aimed slowly, and fired. Notwithstanding the swiftness of his movement, something unexpected suddenly happened. The rock on which he stood suddenly crumbled out from under him, like a clump of mud washed away by the rain. Tumbling off, the man disappeared, and a wall of debris stopped the rest in their tracks.

Thankfully, To-Ho found himself on a crest split by a great precipice, and the tremor did not reach him, but the noise had been so loud that George, wakened from his torpor, moaned in pain. Terrified, To-Ho threw himself behind a huge tree trunk, put the boy down on the ground and bent anxiously over him. He saw that his head bore a wound that bled profusely.

The rock on which he stood suddenly crumbled out from under him.

The ape-man let out a sob:

"Dead! Dead!" he cried out in his language. "Me dead too!"

"Come on, we'll have no such nonsense!" a voice answered. "One dies only when one wishes to. The lad will get over it, and then I'll tell him that he only got what he deserved. Ah! He loves men! They repay him well, do they not? Come To-Ho! To the huts, and move it! I was on my guard, and it was a good thing I followed you. As luck would have it, I arrived in time and my good phobium once again came through marvelously."

And Van Kock, with the wand he held in his hand, tapped To-Ho lightly on the lower back, saying to him:

"Let's be off! Take the shortest way. I will be there at the same time as you"

Then he added under his breath:

"For all that, I do think this will be this centenarian's last exploit!"

Chapter VI

"What the Devil! Did you let them get away? I had ordered you to take them alive, one or the other!"

"Well, Mr. Koolman, if it pleases you to run around this damn country, do it on your own time, and beware these tremors which appear to be volcanic in origin!"

Of these two men one was Mr. Koolman who, to further his hate-driven enterprise, had hired a band of desperados, ready to risk anything because they had nothing to lose. The other was Captain Ned, whom Providence—erring greatly—had just snatched back from the brink of death, as he had rolled beneath the avalanche. Except for a few contusions, he was back on his feet. The dozen or so outlaws who had accompanied them had suddenly stepped back and stared stupidly at this improvised stone wall which had suddenly been raised before them.

It was almost two months since Koolman's group had landed on the Sumatran shores. There, Koolman, had called upon by Captain Ned to reveal his plans. Thanks to the *Porpoise*'s speed, they had a large lead over the *Borean*, which was to bring the Leven expedition, and whose departure had been delayed by the wedding of Mr. Leven with Margaret Villiers.

Their simple criminal tactics could be summarized in two key points: first, to not allow the Leven expedition to be successful at any price, even if this meant murdering them; second, appropriate any possible discoveries made by the expedition, be they gold mines or the existence—which Koolman did not believe in—of mysterious creatures half-ape, half-man.

As soon as the group had gotten over the voyage, Ned had taken command—more in appearance than in reality, since Koolman took all the important decisions. He paid well, and expected his orders to be followed blindly, whatever they were. Amongst those men, there was no one who would balk at committing violence, or even murder.

Endowed with a great deal of energy, further stimulated by his hatred, Koolman, under the pretext of a purely commercial venture, quickly organized an expedition into the interior. He obtained all the necessary information from the Dutch authorities, maps of the interior, incomplete, but showing the central portion of the island and the authorization to request the help of some natives to serve as guides.

Well provisioned and well supplied with weapons, but having, of course, little moral baggage, the explorers got underway. Their route was difficult. Soon, they left all settlements behind and advanced through the deep gorges of the central mountains. Koolman was always after them to hasten their pace. He knew Leven's energetic nature, and suspected that, between his knowledge of the topography and old Valtenius' scientific background, they might manage to catch up.

But if one could get a greater effort out of men by persuasion or threats, such was not the case with the animals which bore their supplies and the tools. Where a man could get through, the Malay horses, regardless of their nimbleness, could only venture with great difficulty. Already, accidents had occurred. Some of the animals had toppled off cliffs with their burdens, and all of Koolman and Ned's furor could do nothing to overcome their fate.

The situation reached a critical stage. Ned was highly experienced in urban crime, where one lies in wait on a street corner, but felt out of his element in this savage land. Its endless solitude irritated him, and, especially, incensed his men who already missed the roads of Holland, lined with taverns where one could have the comfort of a glass of gin to repair one's tired limbs.

A month passed in an unsuccessful search. Koolman, while he claimed a smattering of mineralogical knowledge, had in fact no real knowledge in these matters, and believed that gold was to be found near the soil surface, and that all that was needed for Nature to give up its secrets was a bit of daring and perseverance. Find a treasure, set up an ambush into which his enemies would fall, get rid of any inconvenient accusers or witnesses, all this had seemed easily accomplishable from afar. Now, he began to realize that he had perhaps ventured out somewhat recklessly.

Besides, Ned did not hide the truth from him. Certainly, he was confident in his men, but a man's patience has its limits. The further one penetrated into the jungle, the more distant and the more perilous their return became. Koolman raised their pay, promised larger shares of the guaranteed loot, but even that did not make them any less annoyed with him. Now, another terrible adventure had compromised his prestige and diminished his authority. The night before their meeting with To-Ho and George, the gang had had to face a pair of man-eating tigers. Before they had time to protect themselves, before they had become aware of any danger, one of the Dutchmen had been taken down in mid-stride by one of these savage animals. With one bite of its mighty fangs, the tiger had snapped the man's spine; then, in a single bound, it had leapt into the dense undergrowth with its companion, where they both had vanished. Were the wild beasts going to now join the fray in defending the solitudes that were their domain?

There had been grumbling, cursing, and even the beginnings of a revolt which Ned and Koolman had managed to appease, but things were tense and it would take little to set the men off again. Where were they going? What was their final destination? Could one follow leaders who could not anticipate the dangers?

Notwithstanding his cynicism, Koolman was losing his confidence, but would he ever admit defeat? His instinct told him that, at this very moment, Leven's group, better outfitted, better managed, had entered the mountains. Would he then abandon the game, pull out when success might only be days, perhaps hours, away? Once again, the strong hatred which possessed him lent him persuasive powers to quell the men's remaining doubts, and he consented to the broaching of one of the small barrels of liquor which the pack-animals were carrying.

There was revelry, drunkenness, but also a renewal of energy among the adventurers. The lure of gold was too powerful, and with their brains overstimulated by alcohol, the men had heaped their acclaim on their leader who promised them the riches of an El Dorado to come.

Let's move! Farther still, always farther! Even Ned no longer doubted they would be successful. Forward march!

It had been a few hours after this renewal of energy that they had suddenly seen, standing on the rocks on the horizon, the silhouettes of George and To-Ho. Were they men? Apes? No matter. For so long, they had not met anything but wild beasts in search of prey. But now, one of the creatures was drawing away from the other, leaping with a surprising agility... A certain dread took hold of the Dutchmen, especially when they saw the other, To-Ho, who, in a superhuman leap, had thrown himself into the chase.

They thought themselves attacked by a powerful and numerous horde which would quickly crush them. Their weapons were brought to bear. A volley of shots rang out. Koolman, who had not lost his cool, was screaming at them to stop shooting, to run after the injured creature, to capture it. They ignored him, and Ned himself, in whom the sniper's instinct was waking, wanted to take down To-Ho, the bigger creature, which left itself entirely open, like a huge target.

Then came the shaking of the ground. A dust cloud rose in the air. The mountain suddenly collapsed as if the Earth itself had swallowed it. Ned had been knocked head over heels, and beside him, two of his men had perished in the landslide. The others, terrified, threw themselves back, prepared to run away. Koolman, who, protected by a cleft in the rock, had felt little of the shock now upbraided Ned, and insulted the men, calling them dirty cowards.

But these were in no mood to let themselves be reprimanded so forcefully. They were scared, since nothing frightens men more than to lose faith in the solidity of the ground beneath them. All of them knew these islands to be a land of earthquakes, a frightful phenomenon against which even the boldest men are defenseless.

Besides which, two of their numbers had been buried under a great mass of viscous black dust. Today those two, tomorrow the rest. There were frightful cries of terror and anger. The criminals ran towards Koolman and threatened him with dire reprisals. It was enough! It was too much! They all wanted to go back, to leave this accursed country. But there was more still: they wished to avenge themselves of their discomfiture, punish those they held responsible, Koolman and Ned, his accomplice.

Fear overcame reason. It was in vain that Koolman argued, in vain that Ned called them by name, tried to waken their memories of the struggles already undertaken together. None listened, none wished to listen. A giant of a man, Franz Rod, who had once served a long prison sentence, saw where things were going.

"We must judge them!" he shouted.

"Yes, yes!"

"And execute them!"

In this solitary spot, this small handful of men took on the proportions of a crowd and was stirred up with the same madness. They threw themselves on the two men. Ned shouldered his rifle and aimed, but the stock of rifle came down and broke his arm; he fell. Koolman was seized by the throat and thrown over on the ground. And, running to the horses, others went to get strong ropes, then returned towards the prisoners.

The Malays, who led the pack-horses, seeing the fight, judged no doubt that this was none of their business. They jumped on the horses, and, within an instant, had disappeared into the forest. Such an incident only further stirred up Franz's anger.

"Hurry! Hurry!" he screamed. "Let's avenge ourselves first, and then we'll surely manage to catch up to those miserable Battaks."

Ned and Koolman were each solidly tied to a tree trunk. How were they to be killed? A couple of bullets to the head, that was still the quickest way, and so everyone would have their part in the revenge. Franz split his little group into two. He had them line up at an equal distance, far enough to make the game interesting and requiring some skill on the part of the shooter. He saved the *coup de grâce* for himself. He was a mean ruffian who only found pleasure in crime.

Franz checked if everyone was in place and raised his hand to signal them to fire. Ned and Koolman twisted in their bonds, cursing frightfully. They had their backs against the pile of rock and dirt which had been formed by the landslide. At the very moment Franz opened his mouth to issue the decisive command, an astounding thing happened.

There emerged from the mound, right between the men condemned to die, an arm, then a head, and a voice cried out:

"Help me! Help me! Save me, fellows!"

Franz recognized one of the two men who had been buried, and who, through some unexpected miracle, was suddenly emerging from his grave.

"Lay down your weapons!" shouted Franz.

To shoot at the two condemned men would have meant blowing off the survivor's head. All now recognized their lost friend. They ran towards him and, with hands, nails, and rifle butts, they dug out around him and soon were able to take hold of his shoulders. He was suffocating, his eyes popping out of his head, but he was alive.

"Hey, Peter," they yelled, "take heart, you've come back from Death's door. It's not time to give up now!"

He was pulled from the sheath that held him, and where he had been, the hole remained open. He was laid out on the ground and Franz forced him to swallow a big swig of liquor. Peter coughed, shook himself off, and looked about him:

"Damn it!" he said. "Where am I?"

"Why, among your friends! You can boast of having had a narrow escape. C'mon, tell us quickly what happened?"

The man could not speak immediately, but little by little, he began to tell his story. What had happened? Damn it, it was hard to remember the details.

"It felt," he said with a hiccough, "as though a mountain was dropping on my head. I didn't know what was happening. At one point, I was pushed along by the waves like flotsam, only these were thick heavy waves which were crushing me. Then, all of a sudden, it felt as though something beneath me had given way, like some stones breaking apart or being disassembled, and I felt that my fall was coming to an end inside a hole.

"I was pummeled, pulverized and broken, but not crushed. I could move my head, my arms, and my legs. Where was I? My first thought, I'll tell you, is that I was in a strange moldy, dusty smelling cellar... The air caught in my throat, made me light-headed, but at least, I was alive, I felt it, I knew it, and I wanted it to stay that way.

"Where was I? Well, I remembered that I had a few matches in my pocket, maybe half-a-dozen—as you know, I don't smoke. I hesitated to light the first one, as if I were spending a portion of the life that was allocated to me. First, I wanted to check things out with my hands, by feeling around.

"Stretching out my arms, I explored around me, and suddenly, I was desperately afraid. I thought I was going to die. Do you know what my fingers had met? A hand, cold and stiff. It took me five minutes to get over it. I stayed still, no longer daring to move or to let go of this hand which I felt closing about mine.

"But, I'm no coward, I resisted, I bucked up, and then, having calmed down, I lit a match. And what did I see—statues—big fellows all standing up, and which—though I wouldn't swear to it—seemed to be made out of gold. Yes, gold! There were bright edges, like lovely metal. I lit another yet another match, and I saw more of them, and a number of dark tunnels which seemed to sink into the ground.

"Getting out of there was all I thought of... Was I going to stay there buried among these dead people whose empty eyes watched me? Thinking of the slow, horrible agony that threatened me, I sought to attack the wall, and in one spot, it gave way under my blows. I struck, scratched, poked, twisted, and finally, I felt my arm go through and I shouted as loud as I could, and here I am! Damn it, give me another drink!"

Slack-jawed, the men had listened to this tale, and truly, they thought the landslide had somewhat scrambled their friends' brain. These men were truly ignorant, suspicious ruffians.

"You're crazy!" they told him. "You had a bad dream!"

"No, no!" cried the other. "I saw it, with my own eyes."

"And why would you think he's lying," a voice said. "You know nothing, you understand nothing, yet you dare discuss it!"

It was Koolman who had spoken. He had heard the survivor's story from the execution block to which he had been tied. He sensed that this nightmarish tale might be his salvation.

"Then, if you have understood," Franz Rod said bluntly, "explain to us what all this nonsense means."

"Untie me first, and Ned too."

Koolman's generosity was easily explained: he was better off assuring himself of the Captain's good will. Franz hesitated to give the order to release the two men. Perhaps he still wished to avenge himself of his former frights, but then Ned spoke up:

"Hey, Franz! Get me out of this jam, and I'll do the same for you sometime. No hard feelings, OK? It's just an occupational hazard."

Besides, Franz knew that he might not have had the power to stop the men, whose curiosity was now overexcited and who had suddenly regained confidence in their leader. Koolman and Ned were untied.

"Come here, my man," said Koolman to the survivor, "and tell me all the details. Ned, come and join us."

Peter Gausen—such was the man's name—didn't have to be asked twice and took up his tale from the beginning. Koolman listened attentively and exchanged glances with Ned. They then conferred in whispers and came to a common accord.

"Friends," Koolman said, "I hope that you're all ashamed and sorry for the manner in which you have treated me. I wish to show myself to be generous and forgiving, and I am ready, if you swear, from now on, to submit to my authority, to unravel the mystery which this brave fellow has inadvertently discovered."

He paused, then in a loud voice:

"A secret which will make us all a fortune!"

Until then, the men remained suspicious. They did not believe in generosity. Only the word "fortune" softened their scruples.

"You will need Ned and I to acquire this fortune," Koolman continued. "We equally need you, so it is a pact I propose to you. If you refuse, fine; we'll abandon you in this desert where you will starve to death or be devoured by the tigers. Choose!"

He had been right, as always, to speak loudly and firmly; now, they all began to apologize, begging his forgiveness, declaring themselves ready to agree to anything.

"It's Franz Rod who's to blame."

"You're right," said Koolman, "and only he needs to be punished."

"Me!" roared the man. "Now that's pretty rich, when I could have smashed your head in."

"You had your chance!" coldly replied Ned, who also knew that the power struggle was at a critical moment. Deliberately, pulling his gun from his belt, he shot Franz in the head. The wretch dropped to the ground, dead.

"Now," shouted Koolman, "to work, my friends, and soon, you'll all be rich."

Mastered, excited by an irrational greed, Ned's group of criminals found themselves once again cowering, ready for anything. Ned's impulsive act had chilled their animalistic fury.

"What about the tools!" Ned cried out suddenly, "Those Battak wretches have taken them."

They stampeded off in the direction the Battaks had taken, and there were soon cries of joy. Some small distance away, in the tall grasses, they found the tools of which the Battaks had lightened their horses to speed up their escape. There were handpicks, shovels, and pickaxes. At that moment, they did not even notice that all their food provisions were gone.

They returned, and according to Peter Ganzen's indications, they began the dig. The work was not hard, for it was only a broken up soil which did not hold together, and which could be shoveled away quickly. Thus did they finally manage to clear a large paving stone, which, oddly enough, seemed to be made of the hardest granite, but which had nonetheless, under its weight and contact with this soft soil, shattered into hundreds of shards, leaving a wide-open hole, the one into which Peter Ganzen had fallen and from which he had escaped.

Then, spurred on by Koolman, the men rushed forward, striking in rapid succession, breaking the paving stones which clearly constituted the roof of some underground cave, or rather—as Koolman had guessed—a temple of a long-ago era.

Finally, they were able to enter the mysterious site. Torches were lit, and cries of admiration, crazy whoops of joy, of greed satisfied, tumbled out all at once. They found themselves in a great hall, around which stood an entire population of statues, with, in the back, a throne supporting a huge idol. Of these statues a great number glowed ruddily, like gold. Koolman ran towards one, banking on his experience as a goldsmith, and drew in his breath convulsively.

Gold—it was indeed gold! And in the eye-sockets, on the arms, on the shoulders, on the hems of the clothing, precious stones glittered. It was a fairy tale vision, the expression of their wildest dreams. The men had thrown themselves on the gold statues, to claim them, to roughly estimate their weight. Their motions were so sudden, so disordered, that one of the statues, whose pedestal had been weathered by the humidity, slipped, teetered and fell. There was a sinister death rattle; one of the men had been crushed under the weight.

But this did not stop the others. A madness of fingering, of enjoying this materialistic contact, of feeling the gold in their hands had overcome them. One of them, after a violent effort, had torn from its pedestal a half-meter-tall statue, loaded it on their shoulder and was deliberately heading for the exit.

There were furious cries of: "Thief!" The man was grabbed, thrown to the ground, and trampled upon.

Koolman and Ned were themselves prey to a fever which left them with no self-control. The hall reverted to a state of pandemonium, wherein the basest human instincts were free to express themselves in all their horror. Finally, Koolman and Ned took hold of themselves and rapidly agreed that the expedition's first goal had been reached: there were several million dollars worth of gold here, tangible, cashable. All that was needed was to take hold of it, get it out of this wilderness, drag it to the coast, and load it on the *Porpoise*.

Koolman, using all his breath, managed to make himself heard. They quieted down.

"Friends," he shouted, "your fortune is made, why quarrel and fight? There is enough gold here to make each and every one of you rich.

"It has to be split up!" shouted someone.

"Be assured that it will be shared out," continued Koolman, "in the fairest of ways."

"Equal shares for all!

"Yes, yes, have no fear, since, as I have told you, these treasures are enough to make you all millionaires."

There were roars of joy. Millionaires! This was far beyond their wildest dreams, and from then on, Koolman was obeyed with a great deal more willingness.

"One difficulty presents itself, that of transporting it. We don't have to worry about anyone coming to steal our booty, but we need horses, wagons, carrying slings. All our attentions need to be devoted to this essential point, especially since, once we get back into populated areas, we will have to deal with the curiosity of some, the covetousness and criminality of others. You can see that I'm being frank with you. We must devise a plan together. I am ready to listen to anyone who has some ideas, speak up and we'll do the best we can."

In a few words, he had pointed out the true difficulties of the situation.

"We have to track down the horses and the Battaks!" some shouted.

"That would clearly be the best thing, but they are undoubtedly already far away; however, if some of you wish to form a detail to chase them down…"

Some of them! That meant that, of their small troop, some would leave, while the others alone would remain to guard the treasure! A violent debate soon broke out; knives even left their sheathes again.

"Well," said Ned, "I'll make the sacrifice if I must. You see, I trust you. Besides, is it not absurd to think that those who remain here could take away these huge chunks of gold? Truly, I would defy anyone to take even the smallest of them more than a mile from here. Our friend Koolman will remain with you; I will go alone, with my two most trustworthy men, who will not hesitate to follow me, and the Devil take us if within 24 hours, we haven't caught up and taken by surprise the stupid Battaks, lost in some forest labyrinth from which they cannot escape."

In the unique situation in which these people found themselves—wealthy, but with a treasure that could not be enjoyed here in the middle of the mountains of Sumatra—Ned's proposal was the only one which had any chance of being successful.

A violent debate soon broke out; knives even left their sheathes again.

They had tried to move the statues, but had only managed to throw them to the ground. To get them out from their underground cave, they would need ropes, jacks—and they had none of these. It was proposed that they fill in the cave and return to the capital where they could resupply themselves with everything, but besides the fact that such a trip would take over a month, how would one keep the authorities in the dark about the work intended, and if the Dutch administration had any inkling of the treasure...

At all cost, the statues must be carried to an uninhabited point on the coast, where the *Porpoise* could come and pick them up. In the end, the best remained to accept

Ned's offer and to place one's trust in divine providence for a little while yet.

Koolman was little agreeable to remaining, almost like a hostage, among these criminals who might think to bump him off to increase their own share of the take. But he resigned himself to it; the two who were to accompany Ned were chosen at random. For food, one would rely on hunting and the bounty of the forest, and one would wait patiently, as long as possible.

Ned left with his two companions; his personal interests were his bond.

Chapter VII

To-Ho and George had to return slowly to the land of the Aaps. There, Van Kock examined the young man's wound and ascertained that, thankfully, the bullet had not penetrated the skull; however, while the wound was not deep, it had led to significant bleeding and had greatly weakened him. After a first bandage was applied, precautions had to be taken to not tire out the patient, who, at times, seemed afflicted with a kind of frenzy, obviously caused by the shock of seeing his own kind.

When they arrived at the hut, the good Waa wailed in despair: it seemed as if it were her child again which had been struck down. To-Ho told her what had happened, and denounced men as Go's murderers; the brave she-ape became enraged. She wanted to track them down, overtake them, and twist them to a bloody pulp with her powerful arms. For she felt a great hatred towards these monsters, born from the ill they had already done to her, magnified by that which they had just committed by striking down this teenage boy, whom she loved to the point of having forgotten that he belonged to the same accursed species.

The other Aaps came to To-Ho's mound; they, too, listened to his story and understood. But amongst them, the feelings evoked were more of terror than of anger. A fear haunted them: in the dimly remembered legends of their people, there were a few, barely remembered instances of men hunting down the Aaps, forcing them back, in frantic disarray, into the wilderness where they thought themselves safe. While Van Kock and To-Ho busied themselves with their patient, the Aaps gathered a short distance from the hut and spoke among themselves, with forceful gestures.

One of them, an old silverback man-ape, was explaining something to them, while pointing at the hut with his crooked fingers; grumblings punctuated the more animate portions of his speech, and were followed by strangely modulated cries. The Aaps were twisting their faces, particularly the females who seemed to gradually become irritated, rising toward a paroxysm of anger. But the old Aap determinedly preached patience, at least for a while. Under the pounding of his fist, his chest rang out like an empty drum, and, at the same time, his head was raised in a look of defiance. Just from his pantomime, one could tell that he had taken up the cause of the Aaps, and that he would answer for everything. One could easily see where things were headed once he got involved.

The old man-ape, an elder of at least 70 years, was a giant with knotted limbs, who stood bow-legged on two great pillar-like legs. He seldom consorted with To-Ho, as if an unspoken rivalry existed between them. The fact was that, some time ago, Ro-Ka—for this was his name—had wished to compete with To-Ho for the affections of the then young Waa, who herself had selected To-Ho to be her mate. A fight ensued and Ro-Ka had been defeated.

Twenty years had passed since then, but amongst these creatures still closer to animality than to man, grudges were long-held. Perhaps Ro-Ka had finally found an opportunity to gratify his long-incubated desire for vengeance? The others were nothing more than weaklings, ignorant brutes, ready—all of them—to give themselves up to the latest impulse.

Meanwhile, Van Kock skillfully bandaged George's wound and reassured Waa. All in all, it was a minor contusion; a few medicinal herb compresses, some rest, and the young man would be as good as new. Besides, he was already regaining consciousness, and, not knowing exactly what had happened, though himself to be emerging from a nightmare.

Van Kock, cautiously, reawakened his memories, and George burst into tears. It was nonetheless true that, whereas he was happy and spoilt among the Aaps, and lived a peaceful life with To-Ho et Waa, his human brethren had treated him like a wild beast. They had tried to kill him, and at the very moment when his heart singing, he ran, hands open, towards them, hoping to hug them in his arms!

This was a profound disillusion for him, as if something had broken inside him, and, holding Van Kock's hand, he said sadly to him:

"It is indeed true that men are wicked and cruel."

"Leave him alone with me," said the Dutchman to To-Ho, "I'll calm him down."

Pensive, To-Ho left the hut. He was prey to a painful foreboding, and his great frame was bent over as if a great weight were on his shoulders. And as he moved off, his head down, not looking around him, the huge bulk of Ro-Ka's silhouette rose before him.

The latter only spoke the rough language of the Aaps, having refused to participate in the Dutchman's lessons. His voice was hoarse, hard, his monosyllables hacked brutally short.

"To-Ho, I must speak to you."

"I'm listening."

"To-Ho, we have been betrayed!"

"What do you mean?"

"There are enemies among us who plot our destruction."

"Of which enemies do you speak?"

"The stranger Van Kock, and the young Go!"

"They are not enemies, but friends!"

"You lie or they deceive you. They are the ones who have drawn men here to track us down and kill us."

"You're mad! It's Van Kock who defended us and saved us."

"All the better to deceive you, to allay your suspicions."

"But George was shot."

"The men did not recognize him as one of their own; they took him to be an Aap like you."

Vainly did To-Ho argue: Ro-Ka did not understand, did not wish to understand, and the others who had approached, supported him. It was now the weakest minds which came to the forefront, which asserted themselves. Why had a deadly plague declared itself among the Aaps, if it were not that Van Kock and George, by their evil spells—for these brutes believed in a sort of black magic—had poisoned the springs, the grasses, the fruit in the trees? The she-apes blamed them for the deaths of their newborns; the males attributed their weight loss and injuries to them. A call rose up, decisive, menacing: Van Kock must be killed, Go must be killed.

Then they would leave their homeland. There was another, close by, which they knew well—since they had once lived there—where the solitudes were even greater in extent, the mountains steeper, where man had never set foot. They spoke of Java, which to them was the true Aapland. They would set out swimming, crossing the straights of Sund, and, following the coastline, they would land on a deserted stretch of land, from whence they would dash through the forests.

Truth be told, it was terror which led them to flight. The proximity of man, whom they knew to be close, virtually present amongst them—had the females trembling, lost in lamentations, which only increased the Aaps' fear and anger. Incapable of reasoning, stuck in their simple way of thinking, they wanted to leave, but first, they intended to wreak their vengeance. Around To-Ho, whose more open mind understood their injustice, they jostled each other while grimacing and making menacing gestures.

An animal barely risen above the beasts, To-Ho was prone to mad rages. Anger was rising in his huge head, and it was with great difficulty that he held himself back, feeling that the Aaps might strike him at any moment. If one of the brandished hands were to hit him, it would be over; his animal nature would regain the upper hand, and he would strike back. So he continued to back away, step by step, his fists clenched. A new cry rang out: this time, its originator accused him of having gone over to the human's side and of having betrayed his friends.

Seeing him retreating, these cowards thought themselves the stronger, and as ungrateful as human crowds, they wished to avenge themselves of his superiority. An insult—a certain growl which among the Aaps was the worst expression of disgust—was shouted at him. It was too much. To-Ho suddenly stopped, whipped out his arms with the power of a spring, grabbed the one who had insulted him by the throat, and, lifting him from the ground, began spinning him in the air, striking the congregation of angry Aaps with its flapping limbs.

"To-Ho! To-Ho!" a voice called out behind him.

It was Van Kock who had cheerfully come out of the hut, now convinced of George's recovery and had witnessed the terrible scene, understood, and run forward. The Aaps, seeing him, their principal enemy, to whom they stupidly attributed all the ills and dangers which threatened them, ran forward to attack him. To-Ho let go of the man-ape he was holding, who came to rest in a pile of lianas, and, in a single leap, he ran to save Van Kock. But the latter, having foreseen the danger, brandished his infamous wand, and, before the Aaps, without touching them, he created a shower of crackling, crisscrossing, whirling sparks, erecting an impassable barrier. Suddenly, the Aaps' became so alarmed, bewildered and disoriented that they turned tail and ran off screaming in terror.

The fireworks went out.

"What's going on?" Van Kock asked To-Ho.

The latter quickly explained.

"Bah!" said the Dutchman laughing. "They are just a bunch of overgrown children who will settle down as quickly as they have gotten excited. I will make peace with them."

But To-Ho shook his head. He knew his fellows, knew how difficult it had been to make them accept the presence of a man and a child among them. Ro-Ka used their memories of the tragic events in the gorge to turn them against the Dutchman and himself. Assuming they were to calm down, it would all be a lie.

"So, we're between a rock and a hard place," said Van Kock. "Here the Aaps who wish us dead, and there are men well on their way to reaching here who wish for the same thing. As far as I am concerned, I have no doubt which is worse—I know—it is man."

As he had gotten older, the old Dutchman's hatred of his fellows had become deeper and more firmly anchored. He preferred the Aaps, with their savagery and their spontaneous bursts of animosity, which he feared far less than what he termed man's hypocrisy.

"Listen," he said to To-Ho, "the Aaps have been frightened and they will keep quiet for awhile. If, on this front, the danger is not imminent, such is not the case on the other. The party which took you and George by surprise was not destroyed. I know my own race; they will not be held back by a few deaths. Even after such a disaster, they will be eager to move forward.

"Thus, I'm convinced that these men, after some hesitation, must have continued their march in order to reach our mountains. How many are they? We know nothing of this. What we must to do is stop their advance and strip away forever any wish they may have to venture into these lands, which they must come to fear and curse. I'm going to leave, and set myself to work. I'm still steady on my feed and sound of mind and body. I will manage to discover the secret of their enterprise."

"I'm going with you," To-Ho stated simply.

"Is that wise? What about George, and Waa? Are you going to leave them in the hands of rebels?"

"We'll bring them along," said To-Ho.

"George can't yet walk, or stand anything that might tire him out."

"I shall carry him."

Long did they discuss the matter, but To-Ho was obstinate. They agreed that they would wait for two days and then start on their way with Waa and George.

It was truly a question of life and death for the Aaps.

The others, the rebels as Van Kock had termed them, had disappeared over the last 48 hours, and nothing more was heard from them.

At the agreed upon time, the group left. George was already almost recovered, and the good Waa was assigned to be his body guard.

Chapter VIII

Now let us return to Mr. Koolman and Captain Ned.
The plan they had come up with had worked out admirably. They had tracked down the Battaks, and reclaimed their wagons, horses and tools. Their venture was paying off. With an activity redoubled by the certainty of gold, the Dutchmen used the equipment to clear out the mysterious cave. There was no doubt that it was an ancient temple, a vestige of an era long ago forgotten, perhaps predating all known civilizations. The gold statues were of gods which belonged to no known mythology, the individuals it portrayed being more akin to animals than men. One might have postulated that, in those forgotten times, creatures which were half-man, half-animal, upon which it was impossible to discern where the one finished and the other began, had inhabited the Earth.

However, these were considerations which mattered little to Koolman and his accomplices, as they were not inclined to archeological study. What interested them was that the statues were made of pure gold, and that their mass represented an incalculable fortune. If only they could have broken them up, melted them into ingots on site, they would have done so, but they did not have the necessary equipment. So they had to work in a more rudimentary manner, tearing them from their pedestals, knocking them down, moving them by way of rollers, raising them onto litters, which would then travel, at a horse's slow pace, all the way to the coast.

A Battak, kept in the dark about the work, had been sent to Kotja to deliver orders to the *Porpoise* to come and moor itself at a certain location, where Koolman and his party would rejoin them without drawing attention.

The task was difficult; the pedestal upon which these statues sat was of a cement so hard and so solidly joined to the metal, that sometimes they had resort to gunpowder to free them. Koolman and Ned took on many roles, from mechanic to engineer.

Before the blocks of gold could be removed from the temple, they had had to clear the vegetation around the entrance, open up a path through the forest, cutting their way through with axes and fire. The days went by in an ever more feverish restlessness.

Koolman and Ned were defenseless before a mounting sense of dread. They feared that some accident, impossible to predict, would compromise their work at a decisive moment. However, how probable was the occurrence of such an unlikely catastrophe?

That night, Koolman and Ned ascertained that their preparations were complete. At the cost of great exertions, the blocks of gold had been loaded on strong carriages, some of which would be pulled by horses, and some by relays of men. The road was open, basically easy, with the exception of the crossing of a few steep portions, where one would employ some sort of wood-sledges, as is done in some mountainous countries. Besides, everything was ready to speed up the rafts by towing them.

So, under a splendid sky, whose deep blue was lit up with stars, the articles for transport were lined up across the wide clearing cut out around the cave, within which some blocks lay ignored, some of which they planned to come back and get later.

The men slept. Koolman and Ned, like military heroes on the eve of a great battle, after having long chatted while sipping some excellent gin, of which they had been able to hide a small cask, had finally dozed off.

Nature's silence laid heavily over the place. Suddenly, atop an outcropping which stood out above the others, a shadow appeared, distinct, black against the dark sky. It bent over, peering down, and, holding on to the irregularities in the rock with its long arms, it began to climb down. It was To-Ho!

Some distance away, behind him, in a cavern, Van Kock was with Waa. For days and nights, they had been on the go, moving farther away from their retreat, searching for the men, and until now, they had not found them. That night, they had prudently gone to ground, ready to take up their search at dawn.

The young man had rapidly regained his strength, and was entirely recovered. These regions, with their balsamic aromas, were wonderfully hygienic for wounds, so Van Kock had only had to assist Nature. George knew the goal of their expedition: the driving out of men. He made no protest. In truth, the horror which the Aaps felt towards their enemies had finished by permeating him too. Van Kock had stirred up this antipathy. The old Dutchman was more intransigent than ever, and for him, his hatred of man was one with his hatred of gold.

To-Ho, feverish, impatient, ferreted about, armed with the phobium-bearing wand, and, with a marvelous flair, he would sense the presence of gold, of ores, of even the most obscure veins. Of course, Van Kock, wary of his instinctive bursts of anger, only put in his grasp infinitesimally small quantities of phobium, just enough to disintegrate the gold, but not enough to unleash any greater catastrophe. Likewise, the supply of the dreaded metallic substance which he had accumulated was safe from any search.

That night, To-Ho, who could not sleep, had left the cavern. The air was warm, the sky clear; the ape-man drew in a large breath of the freshening air. Suddenly, he shuddered. Something intangible, indescribable, had struck him. He opened his nostrils and fully widened his pectoral muscles. There was no mistake! It was the smell of gold! He went forward, as if drawn by an infallible magnet. He followed the scent-trail, imperturbably, never deviating from it. Finally, he reached the end of a stone ledge he well recognized, for it was there that he had already met the men, and where George had been shot. He bent over in the soft twilight, and saw. It was the gold-seekers' camp. He could barely make out the bodies of the men, wrapped up in their coats, their black forms arrayed at random. Little did he care which ones they were; the warm effluvia of gold rose up to him.

Then, holding firmly in his fist the wand which held a small chunk of phobium, he climbed down. As heavy as he was, no rustle of grass or tumble of stone did he make. He reached the bottom and then saw the wagons upon which the golden idols lay wrapped in grasses and lianas. But he was not distracted; he did not even ask himself from whence this gold came. It was there; that was all he needed to know.

He crept forward, with the deliberate pace of a beast, slipping among the clusters of sleepers in such a manner that none woke up. He reached the entrance to the cavern, and there, he quickly understood. It was not the first time that he had discovered such ancient caches in these deep gorges. He did not understand their purpose, as for him they simply represented stockpiles of taboo items.

He hesitated. Should the work of destruction begun here? Decidedly not. What was closest to the men should be destroyed first. He made his way back, still creeping and quieter than a reptile, to the wagons. The gold statues were barely covered; they would wait until they reached the coast to hide them completely. He saw the first of them, slowly thrust out the phobium wand, and touched it. There was a very soft crackling, and the gold disintegrated. On the grass, all that remained was a mound of blackish muck. No one had heard anything. He went on to the second, then the third.

He found boundless pleasure in watching the shiny solid matter, whose resistance he well knew, crumble into a moist, impalpable dust. He went on, and on, proceeding more and more carelessly as his triumph went to his head, hurrying, wishing to finish.

"Hey! Who goes there? To arms!"

The repeated cracklings, as quiet as they were, had, by their very repetition, troubled the men's slumbers. A few lifted their heads, saw the monster bent over, proceeding from place to place, squatting down, then getting up again with a happy grunt. At first, they were frightened. These ruffians readily believed in the demons of the night, and satanic legends haunted more than one of them. But the cry of alarm ran out, and suddenly all the men were afoot. Koolman and Ned were among the first. Shots were fired at random, without even grazing To-Ho, who meant to complete his unfinished job. As they ran towards him, they collided with the wagons, and a horrible din arose. Daylight was coming, and its raw light illuminated the unbelievable scene.

What was this muck, this vile, sticky mucilage which replaced the statues, those admirable gold statues? At that moment, To-Ho was tackling the last one, and in the rage which possessed him, he had, in a muscular wrench, thrown it from the wagon. It had fallen to the ground, where its lovely yellow glow spoke to its purity, its value, to the divinity of the opulence it represented.

They ran forward to tear it from him. He simply touched it. Zap! Muck, still more muck! There were howls of insane rage. They did not even think to be stunned, to be frightened by this demonic work; theirs was a rage born of despair. And, in their paroxysm of fury, punctuated by raucous cries, by epileptic-like gestures, guns went off, poorly aimed, striking friend rather than foe. To-Ho had barely been scratched. They were around him, pressing him closely.

Koolman, suddenly thrown into a nightmare, into a vision of Hell, made his way through with no consideration of whom his adversary might be. He leveled his revolver at To-Ho, aiming at his head. Instinctively, as the shot went off and grazed his skull, To-Ho lifted his arm, grabbed the weapon, and, in one of those extraordinary coincidences which cannot be explained, with his finger on the trigger, he turned it back on his assailants, firing off the five shots which remained in the chambers. Ned was struck in the forehead, swore and dropped to the ground. Koolman had lowered himself. One of his men, standing behind him, was struck in the throat by the bullet and crumpled to the ground, coughing up blood through his mouth.

Three other men lay on the ground, badly injured. And the terrifying beast, seemingly belched forth from Hell, swung around the revolver which he now held by the barrel, striking them, breaking bones, smashing heads. They no longer dared fire at him, so afraid they were of this giant, fantastic creature who would not tire. Sudden, a great distance away, very far away, a voice cried out, slowly, in a sound which was both a lament and a summons.

Ned, struck full in the forehead, swore and dropped.

"To-Ho! To-Ho!"

The Aap stood up, and head down, he charged through a group huddled together in the throes of terror, knocking over Koolman who, in passing, fired at him with a rifle. To-Ho tossed the phobium wand into the entrance to the cavern, to finish the work which had been interrupted. Then, reaching the rocks, he climbed up. Ten bullets whistled by. He disappeared.

Chapter IX

To-Ho had easily recognized the voice which had called out in pain: it was that of Waa! Was she in danger? What did this call mean?

To explain it, we must go back an hour, to the precise moment when the day was dawning, and the tall mountain peaks were bathed in the first light. Waa slept deeply, curled up at George's feet, feeling perfectly safe, for the cavern within which To-Ho had sheltered them offered a tranquil retreat. Besides, Van Kock was there, equipped with his infallible phobium, which would overcome any weapons of man.

Towards morning, the old Dutchman had wakened. Like most elderly people, he was a light sleeper and perhaps the scraping of a branch had been sufficient to wake him. Carefree, not even deigning to arm himself with his terrible wand, he had gone to stretch his legs at the entrance to the cavern, happy to feel the rising Sun's caress on his old carcass. He felt happy, forgot his worries and yesterday's anxieties. Ah! Let not men get into their heads the notion of coming and troubling this peaceful setting, for then he would be ruthless. He wanted to end his days in this splendid natural setting, so generous to those who understood its blessings.

He strode forward, head held high, feeling the breeze blowing through his bristly and bushy tufts of white hair. Tanned, sunburned, wrinkled, creased, the centenarian was remarkably ugly: his torso, from which the ribs protruded, was hairy like that of his long-time companions, and, unknowingly, he had taken on the apes' rocking, arm-swinging gait.

Suddenly, from behind the trunk of a gigantic toua-hany, a head popped out, crowned like his own with a huge mop of bristly white hair. Then, it quickly hid itself, only to reemerge a moment later. Beneath the shade of the tall branches, the features were indistinct, the eyes barely visible beneath bushy eyebrows. Van Kock sensed something behind him, and suddenly spun about. Once again the head reappeared and disappeared.

"A *maouass*!" muttered the Dutchman disdainfully. 'That's odd; they rarely venture so close to us."

He began to make his way around the tree. The *maouass* did not appear to wish to be on friendly terms. He backed up, jumping back through the long grasses which hid him to his shoulders. Van Kock understood nothing of this behavior, for normally, the *maouass*, when one walked towards them, would jump up on some tree branch and tear off under one's very eyes.

"What an odd creature!" he muttered, increasing his pace.

The other, still going backwards, suddenly struck a stump and fell, disappearing into the undergrowth, and crying out:

"Damn! This ape is such a bother!"

Van Kock jumped up: a talking *maouass*!

"What ape, you worthless creature?" he exclaimed, answering him for no particular reason.

The other rose with an effort and exclaimed in turn:

"An ape which understands and speaks Dutch! Now there's something remarkable!"

And so did these two men, each with the features of an old gibbon, their hair bristly, their faces lined, stand nose to nose, looking into each other's wide open eyes.

"Who are you, you damn ape, you poor excuse for a *maouass*?" shouted Van Kock while extending his long emaciated arms towards him, as if to grab him by the throat.

"Why, I am no monkey, I am Valtenius... Professor Valtenius, from the University of Groningen, member of the *Artis et Scientiæ Society* of Rotterdam. But you! Are you then not an ape?"

"So you are a man!" exclaimed an angry Van Kock, brandishing the club he held in his hand. "Your number's up! I'm going to kill you!"

"But... why?"

"Simply because you are a man!"

"Are you not one yourself?"

"Yes, I was one once, and like you, I was a respected university professor—Doctor Van Kock."

"The Van Kock who left for Sumatra some 60... No, 80 years ago?"

"Yes—or rather, what's left of him. I have sworn that, while I'm alive, no man shall ever venture into these solitudes. Ah! If only I had my phobium! But, no matter! My grip is still strong and my legs still sprightly. Just wait until I clobber you, vile professor who fallaciously bears the semblance of an ape."

Van Kock spun his huge club about Valtenius' ears. The latter leapt about, protesting in voice and in gestures, seeking to flee, understanding nothing of this scholar's animosity, perfectly willing to declare himself his friend. Twice already, the stick had almost broken his skull, when he was suddenly saved by a diversion.

Waa in turn had risen, and listening, she had recognized Van Kock's voice. What was happening to him? Was he in danger? To-Ho was not there, so it was she who inherited the role of protector. She left the cavern, and ran towards the place where the quarrel could be heard.

"Cut off this damned man's retreat!" shouted Van Kock. But he spoke in pure Dutch, so she could not understand him. Meanwhile, Valtenius, availing himself of the opportunity, had taken off running with all his might!

"He's getting away! Waa, catch him!"

Van Kock ran off to catch the professor, who scampered away as best he could, but who was clearly going to fall into the clutches of his formidable adversary.

Valtenius screamed out with all his breath:

"Help! Save me!"

"Scream as much as you want," replied Van Kock, "you'll be no less pummeled."

And he was indeed going to reach him, when, suddenly, a number of human voices erupted from the depths of the forest:

"Here we are! Have courage! Hold still! We're coming!"

"Damn it all!" said Van Kock with an accent of despair. "The catastrophe is upon us! Men are here!"

In a single bound, he threw himself against Waa, his neck extended, panting.

From the forest emerged a company of men armed with guns. One of them saw Van Kock and Waa, and thought that they were ferocious orangutans who wished to kill Valtenius. A weapon was raised, and no doubt that Van Kock's intransigence would have cost him his life, but for the generous Valtenius who threw himself in front of his friends, his arms extended.

"Don't shoot! It is not an ape but a colleague!"

It was at this moment that a terrified Waa, spotted the creatures she had been taught were her worst enemies, and cried out at full volume her summoning call:

"To-Ho! To-Ho!"

He was the only rescuer in whom she had confidence, her mate, the strongest of the strong!

"But if it is a man, Professor, he should well know that he has nothing to fear from us," said Leven.

One will have already understood that this was the Leven expedition which had just arrived in the middle of these solitudes.

"My dear Doctor, he won't listen. He sought to knock me senseless."

"As I will strike you all down, you lowly bunch of men that you are!" shrieked Van Kock in a paroxysm of anger. "Come, Waa," he said, taking the ape by the arm, "back to the cavern, where, thanks to the phobium, we will be invincible."

He ran off with her into the undergrowth and they both disappeared.

Young Leven interrogated Valtenius regarding the meeting which had so shaken him. Had he indeed just found, in the depths of this inextricable jungle, a man whose name had remained legendary in Holland, the great Doctor Van Kock who, before the injustice of his contemporaries, whose stubborn ignorance denied his discoveries, had exiled himself in such a manner that he was never heard from again.

"Yes, it's him!" replied Valtenius, "and it is one of the most painful moments of my existence that he would not recognize me as a friend, I, who always defended him! He first took me to be an ape. When he realized I was a man, he wished to kill me! It's unimaginable!"

"Professor Valtenius," said a softer voice, "perhaps you yourself frightened him. I'm certain that if I could approach him, he would listen to me."

"Ah! Mrs. Leven, don't take the risk... This man is more ferocious than the fiercest ape!"

"I wish to try... Dear Frederik," she said, turning to her husband, "come with me. Surely, together, we will be able to find this great scientist's lair and convince him that none among us wish him any harm. And then, who knows, might he not give us some clue as to my dear brother's fate?"

"My dear wife," replied Leven, "I'm always ready to obey you, but let's not rush anything for now. It is important that were gather our men, who are somewhat dispersed throughout these solitudes. Perhaps they're searching for us and worrying about us."

"Do so, my love. I have every confidence in you and will be patient, but do place your hand on my heart and see how quickly it beats."

"So it does, in truth! From whence proceeds this excitement?"

"Don't laugh at me, Frederik. You know that women have an inexplicable sense of intuition. An inner voice tells me that my brother is close by, and that if I called him…"

She was abruptly interrupted. One of the men in the convoy was running up as quickly as his legs would take him. He stopped in front of Leven.

"Doctor," he said, "we found a badly wounded man, dying at the bottom of the hill. We improvised a stretcher and have brought him here."

"You have certainly done well. Perhaps Professor Valtenius will be able to treat him in an effective manner. Where is that poor man?"

"Here, a few steps away… We couldn't get the stretcher through this thicket."

"Let's hurry!" Margaret cried out, feeling all the pity which is in a woman's heart. "Let us hurry to help him."

While they spoke and looked in the direction in which the man had pointed, To-Ho's head had popped out above the rocky ridge which supported the plateau upon which the current scene was taking place. Arriving in response to Waa's call, the ape had climbed a nearly vertical slope, and was preparing to leap to the plateau, when suddenly, he saw the group of humans: Leven; Margaret, wearing a sports coat which accentuated her young and slender form; Valtenius, whom he first took to be Van Kock and mentally accused of betrayal; and more still who bore arms. It was the dreaded disaster; it was the invasion.

Where was Waa? Where was the old Dutchman? Where was George? Had they been killed? Men were only capable of committing criminal acts. He thought of throwing himself upon them, of crushing them in a death-grip. No. First he had to find out where those he loved were. He slipped along the ridge, invisible, skirting the plateau, and so gained a location from which, while remaining unseen, he could return to the cave.

He went in. All three of them were there: Van Kock, Waa and George. The latter had just woken up, and, upon hearing the Dutchman and the ape-man vehemently arguing, watched but could not understand.

"What's going on?" shouted the young man as he ran towards To-Ho whose contracted features frightened him. The ape-man gestured violently:

"Man!" he shouted, "More men are here!"

"More men!"

"Yes, our enemies, our persecutors, have penetrated into our solitudes, to bring war and death!" he added, clenching his fists and grinding his teeth. "But not one will leave here alive. Van Kock, we will defend ourselves, shall we not?"

"Certainly!" replied the centenarian, "and should I die myself, it will be the pride of my last days to have exterminated that accursed race!"

"Men!" repeated George, thoughtful. "Where are they?"

"There, a few steps from the cavern."

"Who are they? Are you sure that they come as enemies?"

"Why, are they not our enemies by the very fact that they are men?" proclaimed Van Kock. "Let's go! No more talk! Let us act. To-Ho, give me your wand so I can fill it with sufficient phobium that all you touch will disintegrate and crumble!"

He ran to a corner of the cavern and, from beneath a small pile of leaves, picked up a small box he had hidden there. He brandished it at the end of his extended arm.

"There is in here," he shouted, lifting his head in a defiant pose, "enough phobium to blow up the entire Earth. Let them come and I will pulverize them like the desert sands."

George watched each of them in turn. These savage threats frightened him and he felt in his deepest recesses a certain turmoil he could not master. Certainly, he too was very close to hating men, whom had only done him harm. Nonetheless, a voice rose in him which pleaded softly in their favor. To kill! Could no other solution be found?

"Why not flee from them," he asked. "Are there not in our mountains inaccessible gorges where they could never reach us?"

"And why concede them this territory, which is our domain? They are the invaders! We have every right to hunt them down, and we will do so! To-Ho, can you have a look around and tell us what is going on? Before

217

we leave, we have to know exactly how our enemies are arrayed, so that we can make sure of our strike."

To-Ho left through a cleft in the rock, and, from above the cavern, looked around. At that moment, the injured man they had rescued up had been brought up by Leven's men. The poor man—it was Koolman—bore horrible scars and his face was hidden under a mask of blood. Nonetheless, he was still alive.

After To-Ho's flight, there had been among the men, enraged by despair and frustrated by their sinister discomfiture, a furious explosion of uncontrolled anger. They had thrown themselves in the gold-muck in the hope of still finding a few fragments of the precious metal, and, in this mad rush, they had fought, struck each other, tore at each other. It had been a bloodbath.

Koolman had been the first to think about the cavern. Perhaps the gold which remained there might have escaped the incredible phenomenon? But the least grievously injured had spied out his movements and guessed at his intentions. They threw themselves upon him, dragging themselves, stomping on one another, seeking to tear each other's flesh apart and blind one another.

Now, amidst all this jostling, the wand thrown into the cavern my To-Ho came into contact with the temple walls, and the disintegration began. First, it was a softening, a fine mist fell; then the pulverization accelerated; the ground gave way beneath their feet. The men were trapped into quicksand. Soon, only their chest and arms remained, yet they still fought. Finally, the roof collapsed, and they were buried.

Only Koolman had managed to reach the entrance in time, but he had been slashed up with knives. He had staggered, blinded, shrieking, and dropped on the ground cursing. It was here, lying among the dead, that Leven's men had found him. And now, dying, he looked upon these men who surrounded him and spoke to him.

He recognized them, and all his loathing rose to his lips in a final spasm.

"Leven!" he croaked with a hiccough. "Leven and the beautiful Margaret Villiers, and the stupid Valtenius... Ha! Ha! You think yourselves triumphant... They will kill you! The demons are waiting for you."

"Who are you?" said Leven leaning over him. "You seem to know us well."

In fact, beneath the patches of blood which covered his face, his features were hidden.

"Who am I? The man who loathes you, as he loathes your father, as he loathes that crook Vanderheim who sent you here. I'm Koolman! Who was humiliated, insulted, and who will be avenged!"

Margaret quickly approached him:

"Mr. Koolman, why are you so hateful? I swear to you that my father never did you any harm."

The dying man partly raised himself:

"Ah! It's you, child. Indeed, you're right, I'm going to die, so I should want to be good, eh? You're searching for your brother? Well, he is here. Yes! The natives told me of a young white man living among the ape-men, but you will kill him without ever knowing him, or he will kill you, and I shall be avenged. Ha! Ha! It's so good to die in doing evil."

And the wretch fell back with a death-rattle.

Margaret had heard him. What had he said? Was it true that he had gathered some evidence regarding George? Alive! He was alive! Would he then be found in the middle of these dreadful solitudes, among the strange creatures which inhabited them? Urged on by something which overpowered her will, she called, she shouted out with everything she had:

"George! My dear George! Where are you? It's me, your sister Margaret, calling you! George! George!"

Inside the cavern, Van Kock and To-Ho were preparing themselves for the ultimate battle. The supply of phobium had been split up into portions sufficient to produce its terrible effects. George sat motionless, now fully appreciating the power of the mysterious material. He thought how soon some men—his brothers after all—would meet a horrible death. And he shuddered.

To-Ho, having descended from his observation post, said that the men were many, and that they were young.

"There's even," the man-ape added, "a female among them, with nearly white hair and pink skin all over."

A young girl! Like the one George remembered from so long ago!

"Let's go!" said Van Kock. "No more nonsense. Those criminals will launch an assault on us. They have weapons which kill at a distance, so we must act."

They planned to climb atop the cavern, and, from there, they would rain down upon the humans small particles of phobium. Van Kock had built a sort of blow-gun which could project the material some 30 meters or more. Within minutes, the men would be annihilated.

To-Ho obeyed without question. Waa trembled and kept quiet. They began to climb.

At that moment Margaret's voice rose through the air, screaming: "George! George!"

The young man raised his head, leapt to his feet. That voice! He recognized it, or at least, he thought he did, for it reminded him of his mother's. And the voice, soft, plaintive, repeated his name! Van Kock had also heard it, and watching the young man's features, understood what was going on inside him.

"You!" he cried out. "Are you thinking of betraying us? You'd better be careful!"

"But, it's my mother's voice! She is there, she calls to me!"

"What do I care of your mother and all your family!" Van Kock shrieked. "You shall not leave here! To-Ho, tie him up!"

To-Ho no longer knew what to do, no longer understood. In this confused soul, a battle was being fought.

"Stay with us," he said. "Do not listen to that voice!"

"It's me, Margaret! I'm your sister, George!" said the voice.

"Ah! I can't resist any longer," the young man cried out, running towards the entrance.

By instinct, To-Ho leapt in front of him, his fists raised. But Waa, who until then had said nothing, interposed herself between the ape-man and George.

"Let him leave!" she said in a dying voice.

"No! No!" replied Van Kock, "He mustn't!"

Waa threw her hands around his neck so quickly that he was unable to prevent her actions.

"Let him go!" she repeated.

Then To-Ho moved aside. George didn't even wait to hug poor Waa or to shake To-Ho's large hand. He fled outside. Waa released Van Kock and fell to the ground, exhausted, bleeding.

Soon, George was in the arms of Margaret, of Leven… It was a scene of happiness, of return to human life. However, even among men themselves, ingratitude does not abolish memories, so after the preliminary effusiveness, George suddenly remembered the friends he had just abandoned.

In a few words, he explained himself, skipping over the details. Valtenius, who bore no grudge against Van Kock, was dying to reconcile with him. Leven, thrilled at the thought of having finally found the missing link, was ready to do anything to achieve his goal.

"What must we do?" he asked George. "Let it be understood that we do not wish to use any violence."

George thought for a moment.

"Let me do it," he said. "I'm hoping that when they hear my voice, they will agree to parley."

He took a few steps forward, but he was still some 20 meters from the cavern, when, suddenly, a detonation rang out, dry and brutal.

The ground rose up and stones were scattered through the air. All the men ran forward, but where the cavern had been, there was only a deep, dark, gaping hole, while from one side of the gulf, split by the explosion, a huge torrent-like sheet of water, spurted forth and drowned the stones and soil.

"Lost! Dead!" George cried out in despair.

And at that moment, all his memories of the past, all the evidence of the goodness, kindness and patience they had bestowed upon him came back to him, and falling into his sister's arms, he cried.

What had happened? When his anger had peaked, Van Kock had run to the entrance of the cavern, his arm raised, to blast the fugitive. But Waa had thrown herself upon him, wrapping him in her long arms, rendering him powerless.

The ground rose up and stones were scattered through the air.

To-Ho, disoriented, mad with grief, George's departure drawing out many poignant regrets, leapt to the roof to see what was happening in the distance. Meanwhile, Van Kock, in his frenzied anger, fought against Waa, who would not let him go. Both rolled about on the floor of the cavern.

Van Kock had dropped the box of phobium, his body crushing it. Contact was made. A crackling burst rang out. The phobium scattered, the disintegration occurred, the collapse happened!

To-Ho felt the ground sink beneath him, and, instinctively, threw himself forward in a remarkable leap, clearing a crevasse, and thus was safe and sound—but alone!

Saddened, hunched over, having aged close to 20 years, the unhappy To-Ho went off through the land which had sheltered his days of happiness and sadness.

Men traveled it now, searching, but finding nothing. To-Ho smelled them, tracked them down. Of his fellow Aaps, none remained. All had followed Ro-Ka's counsel: they had emigrated across the Straits of Sund, towards Java.

To-Ho was alone, and remained alone. And so, one night he came to sleep at the foot of a tree. He would have wished to nestle himself in the branches, but he could no longer climb, his strength no longer allowing him to. The setting Sun sent its golden glow through the canopy.

"Go! My poor little Go!" muttered To-Ho one last time.

And he died. Never did anyone find a trace of To-Ho, the gold destroyer.

Valtenius never got over having come so close to solving the mystery of the missing link and having let it slip from his grasp. He mourned old Van Kock whom he had forgiven for taking him for an ape.

Leven discovered gold mines and the house of Vanderheim prospered. George Villiers now held a good position there. Sometimes he thought of To-Ho and the good Waa's sincere affection for him. But it was good to live among those who were his true family, and Louisa Villiers loved him passionately.

Poor To-Ho!

SF & FANTASY

Guy d'Armen. *Doc Ardan: The City of Gold and Lepers*
G.-J. Arnaud. *The Ice Company*
Aloysius Bertrand. *Gaspard de la Nuit*
Stephen R. Bissette: (non-fiction) *Blur* (5 vols.)
Félix Bodin. *The Novel of the Future*
Didier de Chousy. *Ignis (The Central Fire)*
C. I. Defontenay. *Star (Psi Cassiopeia)*
Charles Derennes: *The People of the Pole*
Harry Dickson. *The Heir of Dracula*
 Sâr Dubnotal. *Vs. Jack the Ripper*
Alexandre Dumas. *The Return of Lord Ruthven*
J.-C. Dunyach. *The Night Orchid (Conan Doyle in Toulouse).*
The Thieves of Silence
Paul Féval: *Anne of the Isles. Knightshade. Revenants. Vampire City. The Vampire Countess. The Wandering Jew's Daughter*
Paul Féval, *fils. Felifax, the Tiger-Man*
Arnould Galopin. *Doctor Omega*
V. Hugo, Foucher & Meurice. *The Hunchback of Notre-Dame*
O. Joncquel & Theo Varlet. *The Martian Epic*
Jean de La Hire. *Enter the Nyctalope. The Nyctalope on Mars. The Nyctalope vs. Lucifer*
G. Le Faure & H. de Graffigny. *The Extraordinary Adventures of a Russian Scientist Across the Solar System* (2 vols.)
Gustave Le Rouge. *The Vampires of Mars*
Jules Lermina. *Panic in Paris. To-Ho and the Gold Destroyers*
Jean-Marc & Randy Lofficier. *Edgar Allan Poe on Mars. The Katrina Protocol. Pacifica. Robonocchio.* (anthologists) *Tales of the Shadowmen* (6 vols.). (non-fiction) *Shadowmen* (2 vols.)
Xavier Mauméjean. *The League of Heroes*
Marie Nizet. *Captain Vampire*
C. Nodier, Beraud & Toussaint-Merle. *Frankenstein*
Henri de Parville. *An Inhabitant of the Planet Mars*
J. W. Polidori, C. Nodier, E. Scribe. *Lord Ruthven the Vampire*

P.-A. Ponson du Terrail. *The Vampire and the Devil's Son*
Maurice Renard. *Doctor Lerne*
Albert Robida. *The Clock of the Centuries. The Adventures of Saturnin Farandoul*
Brian Stableford. *The Empire of the Necromancers: The Shadow of Frankenstein; Frankenstein and the Vampire Countess. The New Faust at the Tragicomique. Sherlock Holmes: The Vampires of Eternity. The Stones of Camelot. The Wayward Muse.* (anthologist) *The Germans on Venus. News from the Moon*
Kurt Steiner. *Ortog*
Villiers de l'Isle-Adam. *The Scaffold. The Vampire Soul*
Philippe Ward. *Artahe (The Legacy of Jules de Grandin)*

MYSTERIES & THRILLERS

M. Allain & P. Souvestre. *The Daughter of Fantômas*
Anicet-Bourgeois, Lucien Dabril. *Rocambole*
A. Bisson & G. Livet. *Nick Carter vs. Fantômas*
V. Darlay & H. de Gorsse. *Lupin vs. Holmes: The Stage Play*
Paul Féval: *The Blackcoats: The Companions of the Treasure; Heart of Steel; The Invisible Weapon; The Parisian Jungle; 'Salem Street. Captain Phantom. Gentlemen of the Night. John Devil.*
Emile Gaboriau. *Monsieur Lecoq*
Steve Leadley. *Sherlock Holmes: The Circle of Blood*
Maurice Leblanc. *Lupin vs. Holmes: The Hollow Needle. The Blonde Phantom*
Gaston Leroux. *Chéri-Bibi. The Phantom of the Opera. Rouletabille & the Mystery of the Yellow Room*
G. Marot & L. Pericaud. *Nick Carter vs. Jack the Ripper*
William Patrick Maynard. *The Terror of Fu Manchu*
Frank J. Morlock. *Sherlock Holmes: The Grand Horizontals*
P. de Wattyne & Y. Walter. *Sherlock Holmes vs. Fantômas*
David White. *Fantômas in America*